W9-BUD-264

Voyage to Avalon

Also by Julie Leung

Mice of the Round Table: A Tail of Camelot

JULIE LEUNG

HARPER
An Imprint of HarperCollins*Publishers*

Mice of the Round Table #2: Voyage to Avalon

www.harpercollinschildrens.com

Library of Congress Control Number: 2017938989
ISBN 978-0-06-240402-2

Typography by Katie Klimowicz
17 18 19 20 21 CG/LSCH 10 9 8 7 6 5 4 3 2 1
❖
First Edition

For Emily Hobson,
shield-maiden for life

Lying, robed in snowy white

That loosely flew to left and right—

The leaves upon her falling light—

Thro' the noises of the night

She floated down to Camelot

—*Alfred, Lord Tennyson,* The Lady of Shalott

Voyage to Avalon

PROLOGUE

The waters of the lake stood as still as glass, reflecting the full moon and glittering stars above like a flawless mirror.

The Lady of the Lake ruffled her feathers. She felt the water calling to her, like a forgotten image longing to be remembered. It beckoned, urging her to look.

The snowy-white egret stepped down from the shore. She had learned to mistrust the lake's magic and its unfathomable intentions. The gifts the water gave her came at a great price. Nonetheless, curiosity got the better of her each and every time.

The Lady waded gingerly into the shallow end, disturbing its surface. Gentle ripples formed around her long, thin legs. She craned her elegant neck high to the sky as if in prayer.

"In aqua, verum," she intoned, speaking the words of power and command. "In water, truth."

She plunged her head into the water, swooping down with a small splash. Neck-deep, she opened her eyes.

The water around her boiled and churned, choked with

visions of smoke and flame. Before her eyes, the castle of Camelot was on fire, and ragged, shadowed creatures climbed over its ramparts with ladders and hooks. Behind it, the Darkling Woods also burned. The lake turned a bloodred color, blotting out the vision.

The egret burst out of the water, gasping for air. She flapped away from the lake. No matter how much her wings strained, she would never be fast enough to escape fate: Camelot was doomed to fall.

CHAPTER 1

Calib Christopher thought he knew a thing or two about bravery. In the past winter, the young mouse had encountered fearsome owls, a magical wolf, and the last bear of Britain. Despite all this, he had yet to conquer his greatest foe: stage fright.

The tawny mouse yanked on his crooked whiskers, trying to smooth them down. He stood in the center of Goldenwood Hall, intensely aware of all the many hundreds of eyes staring at him from the stands.

Every year, graduating pages of Camelot competed in

the Harvest Tournament. It was a series of three challenges, each test showcasing one of the essential qualities required in a mouse-knight: bravery, strength, and wisdom.

Calib had faced the bravery challenge last autumn. But due to an attack from the villainous Saxon armies, it was decided that the remaining two Harvest Tournament tests would be postponed until tonight, to kick off the yearly Spring Festival. If Calib passed tonight's strength challenge, he would be one step closer to becoming a squire. Unfortunately, it seemed to take all of his strength just to keep the contents of his stomach *in* his stomach.

He looked at his fellow senior pages who stood beside him on the stage. Warren Clipping's ears twitched with nervous energy. The gray mouse caught Calib's uneasy expression and grimaced.

"After the Battle of the Bear, we all should be *knights* by now," Warren muttered.

"Aw, shut your cheesehole and show some respect," Devrin Savortooth shot back. She smoothed her brown fur under her arm bracers. The oldest page of the bunch, she had more cause than either Warren or Calib to be impatient about the tournament. "Let's just get this over with, right, Cecily?"

Calib stole a glance at the fourth and final page who would be competing: Cecily von Mandrake. Her eyes were bright, and her tan fur had been brushed to a shine that rivaled her slender rapier. Of the four of them, the sprightly mouse appeared the calmest. Only the tight grip of her paw on her sword betrayed her anxiety.

The knights had given Cecily special permission to join the tournament after they decided that her large contributions to Camelot's defense last fall had been her own test of bravery. Calib, too—for valiance in battle—had been allowed to move on to the second challenge even though he'd never completed the first. Waivers to the first challenge would have been unheard of before, but much had changed in the kingdom the past few months. The Darklings were no longer Camelot's enemy. The Saxons had returned. And Camelot needed all the fighters it could train.

"What do you think's under there?" Cecily whispered, gesturing to a cloth-covered mound that towered in front of them, blocking their exit from the arena hall.

Calib, who'd been trying to ignore the odd structure, felt his eyes slide to it against his will. "Nothing good," he said grimly.

Sir Alric, Camelot's head engineer and designer of all tournament challenges, appeared onstage behind them and scurried toward the podium. The white mouse cleared his throat and spoke into a broken Two-Legger trumpet.

"Good evening!" he said. "May I have your attention, please?"

The anxious pages' ears immediately swiveled toward the knight, but nobody else in the hall seemed to have heard the soft-spoken mouse. The larks continued chirping their jokes. The nursery babes shoved and squirmed over one another, trying to get a better look, and the younger pages popped confetti poppers in one another's faces. The cascade of brightly colored paper showered on a few wide-eyed first years, including the new pages from the Darkling Woods.

This was the first time the Darklings had sent anyone to be part of Camelot's page training. It was a show of goodwill—a way to further bond the once-warring factions. In return, Camelot had also sent some of its young to learn from the Darklings. Cecily's best friend, a mousemaid named Ginny, was among the first to volunteer to train in famous hare cuisine. Though peace officially reigned in Britain, suspicions still simmered, especially among the older folk who had spent most of their lives hating one another.

Calib saw Sir Alric's mouth move again, but still no sound came out of the trumpet. Commander Kensington, the leader of all Camelot mice, stood up from the Goldenwood Throne. Striding across the stage, she grabbed the horn from Sir Alric.

"ATTENTION IN THE HALL!" Kensington's voice echoed in the arena at triple her usual volume. Paws went up to ears, but the chatter quieted. She gave a curt nod, then handed the horn back to Sir Alric.

"T-thank you, Commander Kensington." The knight cleared his throat. "Welcome to the Spring Festival—and the final two challenges of the Harvest Tournament!"

Calib didn't like to think about the events of the last Harvest Tournament and why it had been delayed. He still had nightmares about the death of his grandfather, Commander Yvers, and about Sir Percival Vole and the Manderlean—the traitor and the leader of the Saxons—both of whom were still out there somewhere, plotting against Camelot. Fortunately, with the help of Merlin and Calib's new Two-Legger friend, Galahad du Lac, Calib had ensured the castle's safety . . . for now.

Calib fidgeted, trying to focus on the speech that Sir Alric was giving, but his mind kept skidding from one unimportant detail to another. Like how his paws were too sweaty inside his leather gloves or how his throat kept throbbing strangely. He had achieved so much since the last Harvest Tournament. How could he still feel so afraid?

"And so I wish you all good luck," Sir Alric said, wrapping up his words and raising a paw. Six of his apprentices scurried toward the covered mound. The knight gestured grandly toward the arena as his assistants moved into position.

"My apprentices and I have labored many nights to craft a challenge that would truly test our pages for strength." The engineer's apprentices whipped away the sheet.

River pebbles the size of Calib's head had been stacked into four mounds, and they towered in front of them like cairns, the Two-Legger tombstones of old. Calib narrowed his eyes. Would they have to climb them, proving their scaling skills?

"But sometimes," Sir Alric continued, "the simplest designs are the best. The strength task is for the pages to move *everything* before you from one end"—he waved to the pebble mounds and then to the opposite side of the arena, where four circles were drawn out in chalk—"to the other before the sand in this hourglass runs out."

Commander Kensington held out a silver hourglass that looked like it might give them five minutes—at most. Calib almost laughed out loud, but it came out as a squeak. Sir Alric couldn't be serious. The knight was supposed to make the challenges challenging but not *impossible.*

"They must be pulling our tails," Warren said under his breath.

"I'm not going to blow my chance to find out," Devrin said, ears pulled back. She crouched down to the floor. Cecily, Warren, and Calib followed suit. Calib's heartbeat thrummed in his ears, louder than the screaming crowd. His muscles tensed like a metal spring, his training taking over where his mind would not.

"May your strength carry you through!" Sir Alric shouted into the trumpet. "At the ready . . ."

Commander Kensington turned the hourglass upside down. "Go!"

CHAPTER 2

The pages sprinted toward the rocks, and the ecstatic roar of the crowd rose up before them like a tidal wave. Calib focused on gaining speed without tripping, one footpaw in front of the other. Beside him, Cecily pulled ahead and arrived at her first pebble. She cried out in surprise as she lifted it. When Calib skidded to a stop and stooped to grab his, he could see why. The weight strained at his muscles.

This was going to end in disaster.

To make matters worse, the leather gloves Sir Alric had

earlier insisted they wear had no grip. The rocks slipped out of Calib's paws as he ran, nearly squashing his toes when he dropped them.

Still, the crowd cheered, urging the pages on.

Goldenwood Hall's many banners and bright ribbons blurred into a smear of color as Calib pumped his legs. By the time he completed his fourth relay, he was already gasping for air.

He stole a glance at Warren, who had resorted to rolling his latest rock down the arena like a cheese wheel. And even though Devrin was quicker than both of them, she was slowing down, too. Calib glanced at the hourglass. Half of the sand had already settled at the bottom—none of them would make it!

Desperate to move faster, Calib leaned forward and shifted the pebble in his arms—

"Oof!"

Calib sprawled chinfirst into the dirt. The crowd gasped as his pebble rolled away from him. Glancing down, he saw what had happened: Sir Alric's apprentices had forgotten to clear the stage of the sheet, and he'd tripped on it.

Red-eared and fuming inside, Calib twisted and untangled his tail from the fabric. "Merlin take you!" he muttered at the offending cloth.

A few steps away, Cecily had stopped running and turned to look back at him. If it was possible, Calib's insides became even hotter as embarrassment coiled through him.

"Hold on!" Cecily exclaimed, staring at the bunched white sheet, then looking at her gloved paws like she was seeing them for the first time. She began to waggle her paws in front of his nose. "Look! These gloves! They're for *pulling,* not lifting! If we put all our rocks on the sheet, we can drag our pebbles across at once. We just need to work together!"

Humiliation forgotten, Calib sat upright and studied the sheet. And the more he looked at it, the more certain he was that Cecily was right. Sir Alric had even given them a hint: *Everything* in front of them needed to move.

Calib sprang to his feet and waved Warren and Devrin down as they arrived, huffing and puffing from their latest drop-off. "Hurry," he said. "We need to move the stones with the sheet!"

"You're crazy!" Warren said. "That's against the rules!" Sweat dampened the fur on his brow as he scampered to the top of his mound.

"I don't think it is," Cecily said as she picked up a corner of the cloth. "I think that's what Sir Alric meant for us to do from the beginning!"

Devrin's eyes widened as she understood. She threw herself beside Cecily and began to launch rocks onto the sheet. "Don't just stand there—let's get going!"

Calib hurried to join the girls while Warren looked on, clearly torn.

"Do you want to be a squire or not?" Calib shouted at Warren. "We need to do this together if it's going to work!"

"Oh, all right." Warren gave in with a shrug and kicked a pebble down from the top of his mound.

Sir Alric grinned in approval. When Calib and Devrin unfurled the large sheet, he and his apprentices emitted a chorus of cheers. Soon, the rest of the hall joined in.

Calib smiled. They were on the right track!

Finally, after much frantic shoving and yanking, they had all the remaining rocks on the white sheet. With the four mounds piled together as one, it looked like there were enough stones to build a new castle tower.

Calib's heart sank. Even with their combined strength, the task was daunting. The crowd quieted to a concerned murmur as everyone waited to see if the pages could pull off this feat.

"Get into position!" Calib shouted. The mice spaced themselves out along the fabric, grabbing the edges. "One, two, three . . . *pull!*"

They strained at the sheet.

The mound of rocks did not budge.

Digging his paws in deep and grabbing more fabric, Calib pulled harder than ever. He channeled the memory of Berwin Featherbane, praying for the bear's strength. Next to him, his friends grunted and panted.

Slowly, the mound slid forward. The crowd erupted

into uncoordinated chants of "Pull! Pull! Pull!"

"We need to move faster!" Cecily yelled. Calib glanced at the hourglass and tried not to panic. Only a thimbleful of sand remained.

"Together in paw or tail!" Calib shouted the beginning of Camelot's motto.

"Lest divided we fall and fail!" the pages thundered back.

Pulling to the motto's rhythm, they inched the rocks across the arena. Sweat stung Calib's eyes, and the finish line blurred, but he knew it had to be close by now.

The onlookers began to count down from ten. He shut his eyes and gave his best and last heave.

"Three . . . two . . . one!"

The rocks crossed the chalk line as the hourglass ran out and the trumpets blew.

CHAPTER 3

The crowd's cheering cracked through the hall like thunder. Calib collapsed onto his back and flattened his ears against his head to drown out the deafening noise. His paws throbbed. Devrin and Warren shared a rare hug while Cecily grabbed Calib's arm to help him up.

"We did it!" she cheered, her face jubilant. Calib grinned back so hard that his cheeks hurt. Together, the pages walked toward the stage and bowed toward the leaders.

The Camelot larks let loose a shower of white down feathers from the rafters. They fell around the arena like fresh snow.

Commander Kensington looked at the four pages with pride in her eyes. The crosshatched scars on the right side of her face crinkled into a smile.

"A fine display of many strengths, both physical and mental," she said. "And a wonderful demonstration of the strength of working together, for that is the true virtue of Camelot."

Calib gave a wobbly salute, with tail to forehead. He hadn't failed—at least, not yet.

"As tradition dictates, I will meet each of you at the river at dawn tomorrow for the final challenge—wisdom," Commander Kensington said. "Leave your fighting gear behind and bring only your wits."

Sir Alric's apprentices cleared the arena of rocks, using a wheeled tray to stack the heavy stones. Kitchen staff hurried down to help transform Goldenwood Hall into a banquet hall. Tables and chairs made from Two-Legger plates and teacups were rolled in by the kitchen staff. The youngest pages quickly set out forks and knives. Those in the stands began to file onto the arena floor to be seated.

Paws clapped Calib's back as droves of Camelot and Darkling creatures filed past the pages to take their seats.

A beaming Madame Viviana von Mandrake, still in her cooking smock, ran up to shower her daughter with whisker kisses.

"Congratulations, *mon cher*," the head cook said, then she turned to Calib. "Your grandfather would be so proud of you."

An unexpected lump appeared in his throat. "Thank you, madame," he said quietly. He knew Madame von Mandrake was right, but he still wished he could have heard the words in Commander Yvers's own deep timber. His newfound status as a bona fide hero felt empty without the right people to celebrate it with.

"There he is! Calib Christopher!" squeaked someone behind him. Calib turned to see a couple of first-year pages standing near him. He recognized Edwin Scrabbler, as he came from a long line of Camelot mice, but Calib couldn't immediately remember the name of his companion—a young mouse-maid with big eyes and calico fur.

"You did such a great job!" the calico mouse squealed so loudly that many other creatures looked around to see who was shouting.

"Thank you," Calib said. He threw his shoulders back, trying to look more like an almost-squire and less like a lowly page. "Your support means a lot. Er . . ." He frowned. "You seem to have something on your ear, right here." He tugged his own ear, indicating the spot.

"It looks like flour, maybe?"

"That was my idea!" Edwin piped up.

Confused, Calib asked, "What?"

"Dandelion said she wanted to show her appreciation," Edwin explained, and Calib finally remembered who the calico mouse was: Dandelion Fraytail, a first-year page from a Darkling clan. Many of the exchange pages viewed Calib as a hero for saving their families from starvation last year, and Dandelion, it seemed, was no exception.

"Yes," Dandelion said, nodding her head eagerly. "I wanted a white spot on my ear to match yours, but there was no dye, so Edwin suggested flour instead."

Something warm unfurled in Calib's chest, but he couldn't tell if it was pride or embarrassment. Before he could sort out his feelings, Dandelion barreled ahead.

"That idea to use the sheet," she said breathlessly, "that was absolutely brilliant!"

"Genius!" Edwin added, not be outdone.

"Er, thanks," Calib said again, a little unnerved by the pages' fervor.

There was a slight "humph" to his right, and he turned to see Cecily still standing there, her mouth twisted. Calib flushed a bit. She must have noticed Dandelion's floured fur and guessed what was happening.

"The crown, get the crown," Dandelion whispered to Edwin.

"Right!" Edwin rummaged in his satchel. "We wanted to give you something."

And before Calib knew what was happening, Edwin had kneeled down before him, mimicking how knights swore loyalty to their commanders. Flabbergasted, Calib watched as the younger mouse held up what looked like a giant Two-Legger ring.

Calib took the dark wooden ring gingerly between his paws and studied it in the torchlight. It was roughly carved and misshapen. It was—there was no other way to describe it—hideously ugly.

"I carved it myself," Edwin bragged.

"It's supposed to bring good luck," Dandelion chimed in. "Not that *you* need any, of course!"

The two younger mice waited for Calib to put the ring on his head. Calib tried not to make a face at what was supposed to be a meaningful present from his biggest admirers.

"Thank you for such a, um, *unique* gift," Calib said, handing the heavy ring back to Edwin. The last thing he wanted was to be seen wearing such a ridiculous thing. "Why don't you hang on to it for me until after the feast?"

"But don't you like it?" Dandelion asked.

Calib turned toward Cecily, hoping for backup. Maybe they could excuse themselves to dinner, and he wouldn't have to answer. But Cecily was gone. A quick scan of the crowd showed that she'd abandoned him to his admirers and had already taken her seat at the champions' table.

A paw came to rest on his shoulder. "Off to your tables, little tail-biters," Commander Kensington said good-naturedly to the first-year pages. "This champion of Camelot needs to get seated for dinner!"

"Yes, Commander!" Dandelion and Edwin saluted dutifully and scampered to join the rest of the first years. As they went, Calib overheard Dandelion chastise Edwin. "That wasn't what we practiced!"

"Sorry, Dandi— I have a bit of a headache. . . ."

Calib looked gratefully at Commander Kensington, who merely nodded and showed him to his seat at the champions' table between herself and Sir Alric.

Once he was seated with the knights, Calib's mouth watered at everything on the table. Even though fears of another attack meant most of Camelot's harvest was being rationed, Madame von Mandrake had outdone herself. There were salads made of discarded string bean ends and turnip greens. Fresh anchovies were baked into flaky fish pies. And for dessert, candied-flower-petal-decorated fruit tarts made from smashed berries.

Warren held a pie in each paw, and he happily took turns biting into the savory pastries.

"Warren, there's silverware for a reason!" Devrin said,

looking at the gray mouse with equal amounts disgust and awe.

"Oo eeds bibble air?" Warren responded, chewing with his mouth open.

"Eww!" she said, flicking the crumbs that had fallen from Warren's pies back at him. Calib grinned at his friends' antics and tried to catch Cecily's eyes. But for some reason, she turned her head very deliberately toward Macie Cornwall, Camelot's head scout.

"You said something about a new report coming from the Darklings?" Cecily prompted.

The red squirrel took a sip of coffee from her thimble before answering. "I did indeed. The latest report from Leftie does not bode well." Macie was the castle's best tracker, but she spent much of her time now as a diplomat to the Darklings and their one-eyed chieftain, Leftie Wildfang. "The Saxons have disappeared. There's been no sign of them in the past month."

"That's good, right?" Devrin asked, turning her attention away from Warren and his table manners. "Maybe they've given up after that walloping we gave them!"

Macie shook her head. "A retreat would be *something*. But my scouts haven't been able to trace their comings and goings, and neither have Leftie's. Not knowing your enemy's location is a dangerous blind spot."

"Could they be using magic?" Cecily asked. "Like

when they marched on the castle?"

Macie considered this. "We were certainly caught by surprise at the Battle of the Bear, but I don't think magic had anything to do with it."

"When Calib and I were in the Darkling Woods last fall, we saw a Two-Legger Saxon camp," Cecily said. "Only it was hard for us to look at them directly."

Calib had forgotten this detail in all the excitement of Camelot's triumph over the Saxons. "She's right," he said. "There was a shimmer in the air that seemed to block the soldiers from view."

"I'd place my bet that you were just overexcited," Macie said gently. "Shields like you suggest require powerful magic—magic as strong as Merlin's, and no such person exists who wields such a power."

Calib watched as Cecily's forehead wrinkled, and he felt his own do the same. He'd been tired that day in the woods, true, but there was magic still left in the world. There was, in fact, a magical sword in the castle at this very moment.

Cecily opened her mouth to respond to Macie, but Sir Alric spoke up first. "Speaking of strength and power," he said, tapping Calib on the shoulder, "my apprentices and I are dying to know: how did you figure the challenge out in the end, Calib?"

The table grew quiet as expectant eyes turned to Calib.

Quickly, he searched for the right words—the words a *hero* would say.

"Well," he said, reaching for another dinner roll, "I guess you could say the answer was right in front of me, but I didn't see it until I tripped over it—literally!"

Satisfaction warmed him as the entire table erupted into laughter. Calib beamed. Cecily made a funny face, like she'd nearly choked on her strawberry cordial.

Far away and above the din of chattering animals, the chapel bells began to toll for the evening watch. The knights stood up from their seats, and their squires hurried to fetch the knights' rain cloaks. As the knights filed out from the hall, the rest of the revelers stood and saluted with their tails pressed tightly against their sides.

"It pains me to cut the festival short this year," Kensington said to the tournament pages as she stood to join the sentry. "But until we are truly rid of the Saxon threat, we must remain watchful of our walls at night—even if it means making the sacrifice of one less strawberry cordial."

Warren forced a chuckle, but Calib's fruit tart suddenly turned bittersweet in his mouth. Underneath Kensington's joke was a terrible truth: sometimes a knight sacrificed much more than that.

Raising her voice, Kensington addressed the crowd. "Thank you for celebrating with us today and for reminding us all the good that we are fighting for," she said.

"Together in paw and tail!"

The entire Goldenwood Hall echoed back the rest of Camelot's motto in perfect unison: "Lest divided we fall and fail!"

Calib saluted so hard, his tail ached.

CHAPTER 4

After dinner, the tournament pages trudged toward the dormitories, but halfway up the stairs, Calib excused himself, claiming he'd forgotten something in the hall. This was a lie.

True, he returned to the hall, but he hadn't forgotten anything. Instead, Calib waited until he was sure the shrews on cleanup duty for the night were looking the other way, and then he slipped into the tunnel that led to the Two-Legger throne room.

Though it was late, some Two-Leggers were still gathered

around the Round Table. Maps and tokens were strewn about, and the knights were arguing with one another.

"They must be hiding in the mountains! If they had gone south, we would have heard from the villages," one said as Calib skirted the perimeter.

"I've sent dozens of scouts to the mountains," another Two-Legger shot back. "The Saxons are not there."

"Then look again!"

So the Two-Leggers were also in the dark about where the Saxons had gone. This did not bode well. Calib quickened his pace. Still, he was slower than he would have liked. The hallways were filled with Two-Legger feet these days. King Arthur and his knights were finally back at the castle, after a secretive mission. Now, with the Saxon threat, Arthur had called upon the surrounding lands to lend any able-bodied and willing volunteers to be trained as soldiers for the defense.

Dodging an incoming food cart, Calib quickly darted into another mousehole and broke out into a run. He was going to be late!

At last, he arrived at the final bend and wiggled up through a tiny crack in the floor to appear just outside a Two-Legger's room. Flattening himself, Calib squeezed under the door.

"Sorry for the delay!" he squeaked. "What are you doing on the floor?"

The white-blond Two-Legger had been kneeling next

to a door. He held his ear against the bottom of a glass goblet, the mouth of which was pressed flush against the door. The boy turned his head, his gray eyes warming at the sight of the mouse. For a moment, Calib was struck by how similar Galahad's eyes were to those of his father—Camelot's greatest knight, Sir Lancelot.

"Hello," Galahad whispered as he put down the glass goblet. His hand free, he reached for the jeweled hilt of the magic sword he'd pulled from the stone last winter. "Would you mind repeating that?"

Calib did.

"Something sounded wrong," Galahad whispered. Boy and mouse had only begun to understand the powers that came with Excalibur, which Galahad had named after Calib. Chief among those powers was the ability to understand what all living things were saying when the sword was touched.

"There's someone new in King Arthur's study," Galahad continued, voice still hushed.

"Who?" Calib asked. But Galahad frowned, shaking his head. The sword's magic was by no means perfect. Despite their secret nightly training sessions, the best Galahad could manage so far was understanding Calib's *intentions,* rather than his exact words. Most of the time, the mouse found it easier simply to write out what he was trying to say.

Galahad pulled out a scrap of paper he now carried

around for just these occasions, and Calib uncorked a small ink bottle. Stationing himself next to the ink and paper, he dipped his tail in.

"H-O-O?" Calib wrote with his tail. There were always new people arriving at Camelot now. He didn't see how one more made any difference.

"No one seems to know." Galahad shrugged. He held up the glass goblet to the door again and leaned his ear against it. "The guest arrived during the storm, but the rain is too loud for me to hear anything."

"Galahad?"

Both mouse and boy jumped, Galahad nearly dropping the glass at Sir Lancelot's voice on the other side of the door.

"Galahad," the deep voice called again, "could you come in here for a moment?"

"I'll be right there," Galahad called back. He looked apologetically to Calib. "Sorry. We can practice tomorrow night?"

Calib nodded, then quickly scrawled: M-A-G-I-K. Next to it, he dashed off a quick image of a dragon—the Saxons' symbol.

Galahad frowned. "You think the Saxons are using magic?"

Calib could only shrug. He again dipped his tail into the ink, prepared to try to explain what he and Cecily had seen that day in the woods.

"Galahad! Now, please!" Lancelot boomed again, and Galahad winced.

"Sorry," he said. "Can you come by tomorrow morning?"

Calib wanted to mention that the wisdom challenge was in the morning, but the Two-Legger was already opening the door.

The mouse sighed and snuck away through a crack in Galahad's baseboards. He took the long way around to the pages' dormitory, hoping to avoid run-ins with anyone he knew. He'd had enough excitement for one evening.

When he reached the dormitory, Calib could hear loud giggling from behind the door.

"Put it on! Put it on!"

Opening the door, Calib saw that Warren had placed Dandelion and Edwin's wooden ring on his head and was prancing around for the other pages' amusement. Edwin must have left it on his bed for him.

"Go knot your tail," Calib said, quickly grabbing the ugly ring from Warren's head and stashing it into his trunk at the foot of his bed.

"Come on, Calib, put it on," Warren said. "I'm sure you'll look stunning in it—really bring out the brown in your fur."

"Shouldn't you be mentally preparing for the challenge tomorrow or something?" Calib snapped.

Warren shrugged and kicked back onto his bed.

"Everyone knows the wisdom challenge is the easiest one of all. It's just answering questions." The gray mouse closed his eyes, as if he had not a care in the world. Calib shook his head, wishing he had Warren's confidence.

"You don't look so good," Barnaby Badle said to Calib from the neighboring sock. "Would you like one of my cookies? Madame said they were too burned to serve tonight."

The brown mouse had been a page in Calib's year, and though he'd performed well at the Battle of the Bear, one battle had been enough for Barnaby to learn that he didn't want to be a knight. The trouble was, he wasn't sure what he wanted to be instead. He'd been trying different apprenticeships, but none of them had stuck. Looking at the charcoal-black cookie in his outstretched paw, Calib guessed that his stint as a chef wasn't going to last much longer.

"No, thank you," Calib said. "I just need some sleep." He took off his tournament robes and leather gloves and dropped them into the chest, covering the ring.

With a quiet sigh, Calib curled into a tight ball in his bed. He listened to the rain pitter-patter against the roof. From the bell tower, the last peals for the night began to toll, echoing the sound of thunder.

It was midnight, and the storm was getting louder.

CHAPTER 5

Galahad tried to pay attention to his father as Sir Lancelot rattled off the proper behavior for an audience with the king, but Galahad's mind kept flashing back to the mouse-scrawled word: "M-A-G-I-K." And next to it, the dragon. What had Calib been about to tell him? Galahad had never heard of the Saxons using wizards before, and it would take a strong magic to remain hidden.

"Do you understand, Galahad?"

"Er, yes," Galahad said automatically, wondering what his father had just asked.

"That's the spirit." Sir Lancelot beamed. "Then into the study we go!"

As they stepped toward Lancelot's chambers, Galahad caught snatches of a conversation.

"As I recall"—King Arthur's rich voice boomed out with the confidence of a man used to being in charge—"years ago, you refused our offer to train as a page here. And yet, here you are now, heeding Camelot's call for more warriors. You are a long way from home, Mordred."

"Please, call me Red," a stranger's voice responded.

Galahad and Lancelot entered the room at that moment. A stocky boy of about fifteen years stood across from King Arthur. Galahad eyed the newcomer with curiosity. He had wolfish features, though in this light, he resembled a young King Arthur. Shocks of auburn hair curled around his head. Rain soaked his dark-brown traveler's cloak.

He spared Galahad the briefest of glances before turning back to the king, who sat at Lancelot's desk.

"My mother still holds to her grudge, but I am not her," the boy said in the clipped accent of those who lived near the Iron Mountains. "I see the error of my ways now. You, sire, are our best hope in defeating the Saxons once and for all, and I want to train with the best."

King Arthur sat silently, looking as royal as ever in a finely stitched velvet doublet. A simple yet commanding crown sat atop his head. Light streaks of gray were coming through in his hair. Finally, he nodded.

"Indeed, so eager that you couldn't wait until the stormed had passed." A smile began to curl the king's lips, and a soft chuckle escaped. "So eager that you insisted we meet tonight only so that you could ask that I take you on as my squire."

Galahad raised his eyebrows. It was known that the king never took on squires who still needed training. And if he *did* . . . well, Galahad had secretly hoped that it would be him. Only one other person in the kingdom had a sword like Excalibur, and that was King Arthur.

Red shrugged. "Like I said, Uncle Arthur, I want to train with the best."

"I do not take on squires, as I don't have the time to properly train anyone these days," Arthur said. From the king's lingering smile, Galahad could tell he was still flattered by Red's insistence. "However, Sir Lancelot will begin training with his son, Galahad"—the king nodded in Galahad's direction—"very soon. I thought that he could train you at the same time."

"Excellent idea, Arthur," Lancelot said. "I was just thinking that it would be good for Galahad to have a sparring partner closer to his age while we train together."

Looking at Red, Galahad felt his stomach tighten at the idea. Red's arms were defined with muscles, and he had several inches on Galahad. But it wasn't just that Galahad was younger and smaller— He was woefully behind all the other pages his age, having only arrived at Camelot last autumn, at the age of eleven. He was still trying to master basic combat moves with Excalibur.

"My every skill is at your command," Red said, bowing deeply toward Sir Lancelot. He turned back to the king. "My only wish is to aid Camelot in conquering its enemies."

Arthur seemed pleased by this answer. "Very well, then it's settled. Our sleeping quarters are full at the moment, but there is still a room left in the turret above the library. Galahad can walk you there now, and in the morning, he can show you around the castle."

Red flashed a smile and extended his hand toward Galahad. "It's a pleasure to finally meet you. I've heard so many things."

Galahad wasn't sure what to say. He hadn't ever heard of Red—had never even known that Arthur had a nephew. Awkwardly, he shook Red's hand. "Er, welcome to Camelot. This way."

He led the new boy toward the door and tried not to think about how strong Red's grip felt.

CHAPTER 6

Morning found Calib, Cecily, Devrin, and Warren marching out of the castle walls, small, silent shadows in the predawn haze. Calib was unusually aware of his heart. Each beat seemed to say, *Soon.*

Soon, they'd face the wisdom challenge.

Soon, they'd know if they would be squires or if they would have to find a different path.

Soon, Calib would know if this had all been worth it. Even Warren, so confident last night, seemed withdrawn.

The air outside smelled earthy, like fresh mud and

growing things, as they made their way toward the drawbridge. There, underneath the wooden planks, two rows of brightly burning braziers formed a wide corridor leading to the riverbank.

A lone figure stood at the water's edge, obscured by the morning river mist. As they got closer, Calib saw that it was Commander Kensington in a dark sable cloak. A large hood hid most of her face. Without her usual armor, she looked almost unrecognizable. They drew to a stop in front of her.

"Four stand before me who wish to be honored as defenders of Camelot," she said, her voice loud in the morning quiet. "Yet they must prove themselves worthy of this gift and burden."

Calib stood a little straighter at these words, feeling an imaginary weight settle on his shoulders. These were the same words that were told to all would-be knights of Camelot. They had been said to his father, and Calib's grandfather before him.

"Devrin Savortooth, page of Camelot," Commander Kensington continued, "your time has come. Do you accept the wisdom challenge?"

"I've only been waiting for it my whole life," Devrin said.

Commander Kensington's expression remained solemn, but Calib thought he saw a small smile twitch across her face. "Then follow me, please."

Devrin marched forward, her head high, as though she was already heading into battle. Calib watched as the brown mouse disappeared with Kensington into the mist. His stomach churned as they waited for whatever happened next.

Calib glanced at Cecily, who was looking determinedly away from him. All morning, he couldn't shake the sense that Cecily might be mad at him. But he didn't know why. He hadn't spoken a word to her since the strength challenge.

"Good luck, Cecily," Calib said cheerfully, hoping it was in his head.

Cecily sniffed, her eyes sliding over him and somewhere across the moat. "I would say the same, but it sounds like you wouldn't need it, anyway."

Calib took a half step back, startled at the sarcasm coating her voice.

Even Warren's nose twitched in surprise. "Whoa, Von Mandrake, who put your tail in a knot?"

Before Cecily could say anything else, Kensington's shape reappeared. Devrin was nowhere to be seen.

"Cecily von Mandrake, page of Camelot, your time has come," the commander intoned. "Do you accept the wisdom challenge?"

The mouse-maid took a deep breath and stepped

forward without looking back at Calib. "Yes."

"Then follow me."

Cecily's silhouette disappeared into the mist, and Calib was alone with Warren.

"What did you do?" Warren asked.

"I don't know," Calib responded truthfully.

"She's probably just jealous," the gray mouse offered.

"I don't see why," Calib said. "She's the best of all of us."

Soon, Commander Kensington reappeared to fetch Warren. The gray mouse gulped hard and followed Kensington to the water's edge. Calib was alone with his thoughts.

In his head, Calib recited the lineage of every leader of Camelot, from Commander Thornfur the Spiky to his grandfather. Then he quizzed himself on every battle tactic used by Sir Trots the Nimble, who once outwitted three Darkling crow chieftains. The wisdom challenge could cover any subject matter. All Calib could do was prepare as best he could.

After what felt like an entire age, Kensington finally reemerged from the fog. Like Devrin and Cecily before him, Warren was no longer with her. Calib's alarm grew.

Commander Kensington fixed her steely eyes on him. "Calib Christopher, page of Camelot, do you accept the wisdom challenge?"

Sending a silent plea to Merlin, Calib nodded. Step by step, he walked forward toward the river.

When Calib arrived at Kensington's side, he still couldn't see a thing past the thick wall of mist over the water. The mouse-leader looked otherworldly, like the guardian of a mythical river. But Devrin, Cecily, and Warren were nowhere to be found.

"All that stands between you and what you seek is a question," Commander Kensington said. "A question you must vow to never speak of again, and you must answer it correctly. Do you understand?"

"I do," Calib said, mentally readying himself for a complicated question about Sir Trots.

"Which is most important to a knight: bravery, strength, or wisdom?"

Calib stared at Commander Kensington. The question's sheer simplicity hit him like a dull thud to the forehead. And suddenly, he couldn't think of an answer.

He racked his brain for anything his grandfather might have said to him that could have been a clue, but nothing came to him.

They were *all* important.

Bravery provided a knight with the will to act, strength provided the ability to follow through, and wisdom ensured that a knight would not commit foolish acts. How could he choose among the three?

Not wanting to meet Commander Kensington's gaze, he looked around, as if the answer might spring from the fast-flowing river. Out of the mist, he spotted a dark shape on the water.

Calib blinked, but the image did not go away. Instead, it only grew clearer. It was a boat.

"Is something wrong, Calib?"

It took Calib a few seconds to realize fully what he was looking at. And when he did, his stomach dropped like a leaden stone.

The body of a young squirrel-maiden lay motionless in the hull of a small wooden rowboat . . . and the boat was heading straight for the waterfalls.

CHAPTER 7

"Commander Kensington, look!" Calib pointed to the approaching vessel.

It was moving faster now, caught in the current that carried over the waterfalls. If they didn't act fast, the boat would plummet hundreds of feet to the cliff rocks below.

Years of battle experience allowed the commander to take in the situation in one glance. Kensington threw off her cloak and kicked off her boots.

"Get the mooring rope!" she ordered, and dove headfirst into the cold water.

Calib unfastened the rope from its hook on the dock as Kensington swam furiously to intercept the boat.

Squinting through the mist, he saw her approach the left side of the craft. Wrapping her tail around the rudder, she began to guide it back to shore.

Calib paced, the heavy rope pressing into his shoulders as he followed the little boat's path. The vessel bobbed and dipped dangerously as stronger rapids pulled at it. The commander's kicks grew less fierce as she struggled.

With a jolt, Calib realized that Kensington would not be able to make it back on her own.

"The rope!" Commander Kensington shouted from the river.

Calib threw it toward her with all his might, but it fell far too short.

Kensington was now clearly losing her battle against the current, the mist swallowing her and the boat. If Calib didn't do something soon, he would lose Camelot's leader over the edge of the waterfalls.

There was no other choice. He'd have to swim it to Kensington. Holding on to the rope tightly with one paw, Calib took a running leap and cannonballed into the river.

The cold water stung Calib like a thousand lashes. He opened his mouth to gasp for breath and choked instead. His eyes squeezed shut; he blindly pawed and kicked his way up to the surface. He coughed, and his limbs flailed as he tried to tread water. The lack of firm ground beneath him sent him into a dizzying panic.

Calm yourself, mousling. Sir Owen Onewhisker's voice came to him from an old memory. It was of his first swimming lesson, which Calib had hopelessly failed. *Move with purpose, and you will stay afloat. A mouse with purpose cannot drown.*

Calib's heart pained at the thought of Sir Owen, who'd valiantly given his life so that others might live. Calib focused his mind on the dead knight's words from long ago and ordered his muscles to obey. He began to windmill his arms and legs and slowly gained on the boat.

Before he knew it, Calib had reached the mouse-commander. Kensington's kicks were slow, but her eyes still burned.

"The rope!" she called again over the rushing current. Calib pushed it into her paw. There was just enough to loop around the boat's stern. The line drew taut, anchoring them to the moor post. Relieved, Calib followed Kensington as they clambered aboard, careful not to land on the squirrel-maiden. Then, paw over paw, they pulled themselves to shore.

The rowboat hit the banks with a soft thud, and Calib sprang out. Once his paws touched hard ground again, he wanted to collapse from relief—but there was no time. He turned to help Kensington with the squirrel-maiden, but the commander had already hoisted the sleeping figure from the hull and placed her gently on the grass. The squirrel, in a gray homespun frock, lay as still as a corpse. Kensington picked up the squirrel's paw, feeling for her pulse.

"Is she . . . ?" Calib began.

"Alive," Kensington said, her voice rough, "but she needs a healer. Grab her arms— Let's take her to the council room!"

Calib did as he was told. His muscles protested under the weight, but between the two mice, they were able to carry the unconscious squirrel. Together, they took the quickest way back to the castle, tracing a path to the council room.

While Goldenwood Hall was considered the heart of Camelot, the small council room was the brain. Here, a large round platter over an empty spool served as a mouse-sized Round Table. Scores of overturned cups lined the edge for seating.

As they entered the room, Calib was startled by a burst of applause. The beaming faces of Warren and Devrin greeted him while even Cecily managed a small, tight smile. But as their new visitor became visible behind him, their clapping cut short.

"Where's Viviana?" Commander Kensington asked through gritted teeth, wobbling a little. "And someone fetch Macie!"

Cecily sprinted from the room while Warren and Devrin ran forward to assist Commander Kensington. They lifted the squirrel onto the table.

"Is she dead?" Warren asked, looking like he might pass out if the answer was yes.

"Not if we can help it," Kensington replied. She took off her sable cloak and tucked it around the wet squirrel.

"What *happened*?" Devrin asked. As they waited, Calib recounted their adventure on the river.

"Move aside," Viviana von Mandrake said sharply, appearing with a stash of herbs she kept draped across her chest at all times. "Give the poor thing some air."

Calib scrambled to obey. The head chef was the closest they had to a healer, since the traitor Sir Percival Vole had joined the Saxons. Before arriving at Camelot, Madame had run an inn and knew how to care for minor cuts and rashes procured while traveling.

"Can you help?" Commander Kensington asked.

"Perhaps, but this is beyond my training." Madame von Mandrake felt the squirrel's forehead. "We need to find a proper healer."

"We'll send a message to our Darkling allies, then," Kensington said.

Tsking softly, Madame von Mandrake pulled some foul-smelling weeds from her sash. She held them close against the squirrel's nose.

For a moment, nothing happened, and an awful chill

seemed to settle in Calib's gut. But then, the maiden stirred ever so slightly, her eyelids fluttering. Calib thought he saw her mouth move.

"What's she saying?" Kensington asked.

Madame von Mandrake looked at the commander, wide-eyed. "She's saying 'Avalon.'"

The name trickled through the group in burbling murmurs.

For most woodland creatures, Avalon was a myth passed down by nursery maids and bards. They spoke of a magical island somewhere in the Sapphire Sea, enshrouded by mist and protected by the highest order of magic left on this Earth. It was said that its mysterious inhabitants, the Silent Sisters, possessed the power to tell the future and heal all illnesses.

But though many spoke of it, no one had ever been able to give an accurate account of its location. And thus, the island was not marked on any map.

Madame von Mandrake held more herbs under the squirrel's nose, and this time, Calib learned forward to hear what the squirrel said before she passed out again:

"Too late . . . too late."

CHAPTER 8

Galahad's stomach growled like an ornery troll, or at the very least, a troll who had missed breakfast and was so hungry he was ready to eat his own shoes. Because that's exactly how Galahad was feeling now, and it was all Red's fault.

Red had been late meeting him, which meant they had both missed breakfast.

"As you can see," Galahad said stiffly, "you'll want to show up early. The food is usually cold and picked over within the hour." He waved at the tables in the dining hall, still lined with crumbs from that morning's breakfast.

Red ducked his head. "Sorry about that," he said. "I got lost coming here. The castle is just so very big."

The hungry troll living in Galahad's stomach couldn't imagine what path Red could have taken to make him as late as he was, but the part of Galahad that remembered his own arrival the past fall felt a pang of sympathy for the newcomer.

"It takes some getting used to," Galahad admitted. The stone castle had felt cold and intimidating compared to St. Anne's sunlit cloisters, where Galahad had lived with his mother, Lady Elaine, and had learned to read and write. It was only now, several months later, that Camelot was finally starting to feel like home.

"This way," Galahad said. "We can go to the cellar and maybe swipe some cheese and bread."

Red followed on Galahad's heels as the younger boy showed him through the doors.

"I'm eager to spar tomorrow," Red said. "I've never had to duel against a legendary sword like Excalibur!"

"We train with wooden ones first."

"Ah, I guess that's not as exciting." Red looked crestfallen at this news. "I've heard so much about your sword."

"Really?" Galahad said, wariness nipping at the back of his mind. These days, what most people heard about Galahad and Excalibur were outright exaggerations. Depending on whom you asked, Galahad had trained circus animals to attack the Saxons or he had pulled the sword out of the stone using black magic.

"That must have been some powerful spell you used on the Sword in the Stone," Red continued. "A great wizard must have taught you. My mother, Morgan le Fay, trained with Merlin once. Who did you learn from?"

Galahad shrugged, uncomfortable. He'd had no training, and his only help had come from a mouse. "I was just there at the right time," he said carefully—and truthfully. Because he didn't have an answer. He just knew that Calib and his friends had had something to do with it.

Red didn't look like he believed Galahad, but he dropped the subject. Galahad led them down a long spiraling staircase that opened on a network of tunnels and caves. Most of them contained Camelot's food stores, which allowed the castle dwellers to outlast the winter.

In the distance, they could hear the rhythmic hammering of carpenters. King Arthur was having more shelves built into the farther reaches of the caves. He wanted to double their supplies in case of a siege.

"Legend has it the caves were created by a dragon burrowing deep underneath this castle. And these cellars are just a small fraction of how deep the tunnels go," Galahad said. He cracked open a box full of crusty bread and broke off a hunk to give to Red.

"Sounds like a good place to bury treasure . . . or hide bodies," Red said, taking a wolfish bite.

"I haven't found either," Galahad said, though his thoughts flew to the secret tunnel that led below the cliffs.

From far away, the chapel bells began to toll. Galahad uttered a silent curse. It was already midmorning. He wouldn't be able to meet Calib now until the evening. He'd promised he'd meet the castle healer, Father Walter, in the apothecary to go over the medicinal supplies before training with his father in the afternoon.

Galahad quickly stuffed some cheese into his pocket and turned toward the exit. "I, um, need to run a few errands. Do you want me to show you back to the library?"

"I think I'm all right down here," Red replied, distracted. He was running his hands along the stalagmites, the stores of food forgotten.

"As you will," Galahad said, and began to leave the cellars. But before he headed up the stairs, Galahad looked back in time to see Red disappear into the caves.

CHAPTER 9

As quickly as the squirrel had awoken, she slipped into another feverish sleep. Calib watched anxiously as Madame von Mandrake examined under the squirrel's eyelids and placed a cold rag on her forehead. The squirrel's gray-brown fur was matted in dirty clumps, and her dress was caked with mud.

"The poor thing must have traveled through the storm last night. She's dehydrated and running a high fever," Madame von Mandrake said.

"What can we do?" Calib asked helplessly. He felt

strangely responsible for this creature he'd helped fish out of the river.

"Let me see her."

Calib looked up to see Macie Cornwall enter the room at that moment, and he felt a small pinch of relief. If anyone might be able to recognize the new arrival, she would. Breaking through the circle, she studied the squirrel's features.

"I don't know her by name," Macie said, "but her dress and fur color suggest that she's from the Pawhill clan near the Iron Mountains." She looked up at the small group, her face sad. "She's far from home."

"We ought to move her somewhere more comfortable," Commander Kensington said, and Madame nodded her head in agreement.

"What do we think she meant by 'too late'?" Calib asked. "And why would she speak of Avalon?" He shivered, but he wasn't sure if it was from his still-drenched fur or from the squirrel-maiden's words.

"Unless we break her fever, we won't get a chance to ask," Madame von Mandrake said, eyes grim.

"Is there anything we can do to help?" Cecily asked her mother.

Madame tilted her head, thinking for a moment. "Remember when those hedgehog travelers came to the inn with their little one suffering from sea fever?"

Cecily's whiskers twitched in concentration. "You used crushed feverfew blossoms in a tea for him, right?"

The elder Von Mandrake nodded. "I could do the same here, but we used up all our supply during the Battle of the Bear."

"I could look in the Two-Legger infirmary; they may have a few left," Calib suggested, accidentally volunteering himself.

"Good idea," Commander Kensington said. "You and Cecily investigate and see what you find."

Cecily wrinkled her snout but didn't say anything as she turned to leave the council room. Calib had to sprint to catch up with her.

They began their journey to the Two-Legger infirmary, which was located past the chapel, in the west end of the castle. They wound the well-trod path underneath the chapel's pews.

As they traveled, he racked his brain for something interesting to say. Nothing came to mind.

"Congratulations, by the way." Cecily finally broke the silence herself. "On passing the final challenge."

"Actually, I'm not so sure if I *did*," Calib said. "I didn't give an answer yet."

"Well, it's not like the challenge really matters," Cecily said. "Commander Kensington wouldn't let the 'great hero' of Camelot fail, would she?"

Something about Cecily's tone made Calib feel defensive. "What's that supposed to mean?" he said. "You think I don't deserve to be a squire?"

"No, I don't mean that, but . . ." Cecily scrunched her forehead together. "It's just . . . You have your own fan club, for Merlin's sake! Dandelion's so besotted, she doesn't speak of anything else. And all Edwin ever talks about is learning fencing skills from *you!*"

"You think I *want* all this attention?" Calib sputtered.

Cecily stopped and whirled on Calib. "I mean, *I'm* the one who taught Edwin how to feint and riposte properly. And as I recall, *two* of us went on a journey to save Camelot, but to hear anyone speak of it, it sounds like a one-mouse show!"

"I can't control what creatures say," Calib said, crossing his arms.

Cecily narrowed her eyes, her paws clenched together into fists. "Oh really? Because back there during the strength challenge, you were more than eager to take credit for *my* idea."

Now Calib was mad.

"That was a group effort!" he said. "You wouldn't have thought of the solution if I hadn't tripped on the sheet in the first place."

"And what great skill and training *that* took!" Cecily quickened her pace, her tail tip whipping in front of

Calib's nose while he reeled with anger and confusion. They lapsed into a silence even more awkward than before as they ran up a wooden truss leading to the infirmary. Long wooden beams crisscrossed the room, holding up thick curtains that separated the beds.

Calib and Cecily tiptoed across the beams to reach the apothecary shelves on the far wall. The shelves were filled with colorful jars of every shape and size containing herbs and potions, salves and ointments.

Weaving in and out of the bottles, they sniffed each one for the bitter scent of feverfew.

"Over here!" Cecily pointed to a tall, green glass bottle on the shelf below them. A few dried petals and stems lay crumpled inside. "I think that's it."

Tightly gripping the edge of the shelf, the two mice carefully lowered themselves. Calib's arms, still sore from the strength challenge, throbbed in protest. Dropping the remaining distance, Cecily landed nimbly while Calib fell on his rear with a thump.

Cecily glared at him. "Do you mind? We're trying to be stealthy here." She gave the feverfew bottle a few test pushes. Calib set his paws besides hers to help, but the bottle was much heavier than Calib thought. It would take both of them to get it on its side.

"Here, I'll push, and you'll catch it," Cecily said.

Just as the two mice readied the bottle for tipping,

they heard a pair of voices approaching. Soft Two-Legger footsteps followed, and the torchlights in the hall flickered from the passing movement. Calib and Cecily hid behind the feverfew bottle as two large Two-Legger shadows fell on them.

To Calib's relief, he saw that one of them belonged to Galahad. The other belonged to Camelot's head healer, Father Walter, a frail but wise old monk who limped around with a cane. His eyesight was poor, but his knowledge of the healing arts was unparalleled.

"Let's see," the old man said, squinting at the shelves. "I believe these mudberry salves can go back to the cellar next."

"Mudberry," Galahad echoed. "But isn't that a poison, causing fever and hallucinations?"

"You're a fast learner," Walter said, nodding in approval. "Mudberry is indeed poisonous if you eat it, but if applied to the skin, it simply numbs pain."

"I see," Galahad said. Calib watched as he pulled some of the jars from the shelves, his hand creeping nearer to their hiding place.

"It's a shame you aren't training to be a healer." Father Walter sighed, returning his attention to the shelves. Cecily and Calib shrank farther back. "It's easier to swing a sword than to try to fix the damage it does."

"I know," Galahad said, and from the shadow in the

boy's tone, Calib knew he was thinking of all the warriors who had yet to recover from their injuries.

The healer must have understood too, because he nodded and patted Galahad's shoulder.

"Well, let's see what I can teach you before your training starts again. Today, let's go over the healing properties of feverfew."

Calib's heart beat faster than a sprinting hare's, as he watched the older Two-Legger began to skim the labels on the jars. Calib wished Galahad would brush his hand on Excalibur so he could speak a message.

"Now where did I put it . . . ," the old man mumbled.

Calib nudged Cecily. "We need to go."

Cecily shook her head. "Don't be a 'fraidy mouse; we can do this," she said. She began to push the glass bottle in an effort to tip it toward Calib so he could catch it.

But as it fell, he lost his grip. Slowly, the vessel rolled along its bottom edges in an arc away from them.

"No, no, no, no, no," Cecily said through gritted teeth, trying to hold it back.

But the weight was too much.

The bottle toppled over the edge of the shelf, and with a sound like splintering ice, it shattered into hundreds of pieces.

CHAPTER 10

"By Merlin, what was that?!" exclaimed Father Walter, blinking. He squinted at the broken glass.

Calib waved a weak hello to Galahad, whose eyes widened when he spotted the two mice on the shelf.

"Nothing! I just knocked over a bottle—being clumsy!" Galahad said. "I'll get the broom."

The boy quickly scooped up both of the mice and shoved them into his pocket, which smelled slightly of cheese. Cecily's paw darted for her rapier, but Calib caught her wrist first.

"He's an ally, remember?"

The world rocked as the boy moved. Calib and Cecily bumped against each other in the dark, and Calib was glad he hadn't had the chance to eat breakfast. He didn't want to reward his friend for saving their tails with a pocketful of mouse sick.

Galahad's hand suddenly appeared.

"Okay," the boy whispered. "You can come up now."

Calib and Cecily poked their heads out of Galahad's pocket. Following Calib's lead, Cecily clambered onto the boy's forearm and looked around. They were in a broom closet, safely hidden from Father Walter's view.

"You could have just asked, you know," Galahad said good-naturedly. He placed the palm of his hand on Excalibur to better understand the mouse's response.

"There wasn't any time," Calib squeaked. He tried to convey to Galahad the emergency as best he could. He mimicked falling ill by placing the back of his paw on his forehead and pretending to faint.

"Someone's sick?" Galahad guessed, furrowing his brows in concentration.

Calib nodded, ignoring Cecily's sharp intake of breath. "Did he just *understand* you?" she hissed, wide-eyed, like Calib had sprouted a unicorn horn.

Calib winced, knowing he'd have some explaining to do later, but also knowing that a creature's life hung in the balance.

"Yes," he said in response to both Galahad's and

Cecily's questions.

"I'll fetch something to help," Galahad said. "You and your friend should keep your heads down; it could get bumpy."

Calib and Cecily were once again jostled back and forth in Galahad's pocket as he returned to the infirmary with the broom. They could hear Galahad hastily sweeping up the broken jar.

Cecily turned to Calib with fury in her eyes, and gave him a big shove. "And when were you going to tell me that you could talk to Two-Leggers?" she demanded.

Calib couldn't seem to do anything right. "I'm sorry, but we thought it would be safer if people didn't know."

"Oh, now you're keeping secrets from your own kind." Cecily crossed her arms.

"We're all a part of Camelot—not just the mice," Calib said. "We should be working together!"

Suddenly, the pocket opened from above and wads of feverfew fell around them. Cecily brusquely pushed herself off Calib and collected the blossoms into her bag.

"I should put this broken glass out for the blacksmith to collect and remelt," Calib heard Galahad say to Father Walter. He felt the shifts in movement as Galahad walked into the main infirmary.

Once outside, the mice climbed out of Galahad's pocket and onto his open palm. Galahad's hand shook a little, and

Calib thought that their paws must tickle his skin. Even so, the boy carefully helped them to the ground.

"I need to get back to Father Walter before he suspects anything," Galahad said.

"Thank you," Calib said. "You're a mouse among men."

Galahad grinned wide, and Calib could tell this was one of the rare times when Excalibur had translated exactly what he meant. "That's the best compliment anyone has ever given me," the boy replied.

When Cecily and Calib arrived back at the council room, they found that the space had been turned into a makeshift sickroom. A bed of seat pillows had been placed underneath the squirrel. A tapestry had been taken down to use as a blanket. Warren and Devrin gently blew on a small fire while Madame von Mandrake and Kensington remained around the squirrel.

"Everything went smoothly?" Commander Kensington asked, looking up.

Nervously, Calib glanced at Cecily. What if Cecily was angry enough to expose his secret?

Cecily paused for a moment, then nodded, bringing out the wad of feverfew blossoms from her satchel. "Everything went smoothly, Commander."

Calib breathed a sigh of relief. Madame von Mandrake took the blossoms and put them in a kettle she had been brewing in the fireplace. Devrin hurried to stir the flames.

"Will this work?" Kensington said.

"I'm no healer, Commander. My skills are limited," Madame von Mandrake said, her nose twitching. "The only one who could say for sure . . . We wouldn't want his help, anyway."

Thoughts of Sir Percival, Camelot's former healer, left a sour taste in Calib's mouth. Using a reed as a straw, Madame von Mandrake siphoned a few droplets from the tea and let them trickle down the squirrel's open mouth.

Even after a few breathless seconds, nothing seemed to happen.

"Maybe it doesn't work on animals," Cecily ventured.

Suddenly, the squirrel-maiden jerked awake. She yelped at the top of her lungs as she thrashed. Commander Kensington and Madame von Mandrake grabbed her arms so she would not injure herself.

"It's all right!" Calib said. "You're safe now!"

Slowly, the visitor began to calm, and she looked around with wide, frightened eyes.

Calib offered her some more of the feverfew tea. After hesitating, she took it gratefully, and finally let her surroundings sink in.

"Where am I?" she asked between sips.

"Camelot," Kensington said. "We fished you out of the river right before your boat went over the waterfalls. I am

Commander Kensington. And you are?"

The squirrel's face dropped, and for a moment, Calib thought she might cry. Instead, she tried to stand up.

"My name is Saffron Pawhill," the squirrel said, setting aside the tea and struggling to rid herself of the blanket. "I must have taken a wrong turn at some point upstream. Thank you for your hospitality, but I really must be going now."

"*Alors*, you're not going anywhere," Madame von Mandrake chided. "You were half dead when we found you, and you have much resting to do."

She tried to pat Saffron's paw, but the squirrel quickly pulled the blanket over her body. Her fever-bright eyes filled with tears.

"But I can't stay! I'm putting you all in danger just by being here," Saffron said, bursting into sobs. "I must find Avalon before it's too late!"

Avalon again. Calib felt the fur on the nape of his neck rise, as though magic had brushed against it. Warren too seemed affected by the word. He shifted uneasily by the fireplace.

"Avalon?" Kensington asked, and Calib was impressed by the commander's calmness. "Why are you trying to get there?"

"A terrible disease has taken hold of our village, m'lady," Saffron responded, drying her eyes on the edge of the blanket. "Like nothing that we've seen before. We were getting desperate."

Everyone in the room shifted uncomfortably as they realized why Saffron did not want to be touched.

"Tell us everything," the mouse-commander ordered, the scars on her snout seeming to deepen in the flickering light of the fire.

"The fever set in before the snow had fully melted," Saffron began. "We'd just had a terrible winter, and everyone was eager to celebrate the warmer season. We decided to host our Spring Fair a few weeks early. It was a wonderful evening, full of dancing, storytelling, and roasted acorns. There was even a traveling band of bards who sang the night away."

A ghost of a smile played beneath Saffron's snout as she described the memory. "But the next day, a few of the elders were complaining of headaches and dizziness. The day after that, the fever and chill set in.

"Then a few days after that, all the adults in our village fell into a deep sleep and would not wake up."

Saffron lifted her luminous eyes to the crowd. "We tried to contain it; honest we did. But the illness spread, no matter how quickly and carefully we quarantined the sick. And after my own da, the town healer, fell to it, well . . . . we just didn't know what else to do. And so I set off for Avalon . . ." Saffron's voice trailed off.

"It sounds like sea fever," Madame said gravely.

The words struck a cold chord in Calib's chest. His mother, among many others, had passed away from sea fever when he was just a babe. Since the castle sat so close to the ocean, the sickness was a part of life. But Lady Clara Christopher had only recently lost Calib's father in the Great War between Camelot and the Darklings, and the illness had proved too much for her.

"But sea fever as far inland as the Darkling forest?" Madame von Mandrake said. "That's unheard of."

"We must warn the other villages in that area," Macie said. The squirrel's tail had puffed up in her agitation. "Has your clan traveled anywhere else?"

Saffron shook her head. "No. As soon as Elder Pawhill fell ill, we forbade anyone from leaving."

"Then we still have time to warn the neighboring villages," Macie said.

"But what does it mean for us, right here, right now?" Madame von Mandrake asked. "Sea fever is highly contagious. The infirmary is not supplied for something like this."

"Let's not panic when there is still much we do not know," Kensington said calmly. "We will, however, err on the side of caution. All of us who have touched Saffron will be in quarantine for a brief time until we know more."

"Quara-what?" Warren asked.

"Quarantine, *mon petit chou-fleur,*" Madame Von Mandrake said, "is when the creatures who have been exposed to illness stay away from the animals who have not."

Commander Kensington nodded. "All creatures who have touched Saffron—Madame, Calib, Warren, Devrin, and myself—must stay inside the council room until further notice. We cannot risk spreading the disease to others."

Warren and Devrin looked at their paws, as if they wanted to scrub them, while Cecily looked at her friends, horrified. Out of the pages, she was the only one who had not helped lift Saffron. Calib's breath caught in his throat. He heard what Kensington had left unsaid: a new, invisible enemy had entered the castle.

CHAPTER 11

That evening, Galahad couldn't sleep. Calib hadn't come for their nightly practice session with Excalibur, and he wondered if the feverfew had helped whoever was sick.

Spring was an odd time of year for sickness to strike, especially from the Darkling Woods. He wondered if others in Britain had noticed this, too.

Throwing off his covers, Galahad snuck out of bed and pulled on a cloak. Silent as a shadow, he made his way to the tower.

In the aviary, he quickly scratched three messages onto

pieces of parchment and sealed them shut with a wax seal bearing the sigil of Camelot's healer. Each of the messages said the same thing: *Signs of sickness?*

He attached the scrolls to different messenger larks, directing them in three different points toward the west. As they took off, Galahad hoped they would take with him the worried pressure that stayed on his chest. But as the birds disappeared into the slowly graying sky, the weight only seemed to increase.

"What are you doing?"

The unexpected voice behind Galahad made him jump, and he whirled around to see Red, fully dressed. His eyes were alert, as though he'd been up for hours.

"Sending a message to my, uh, mother," Galahad said. The lie squirmed inside him, but he tried to keep his face blank. No one knew that he could speak with animals, and he didn't feel like explaining until he understood it more. After all, who would believe him?

Red remained silent, looking intently at him.

"What are *you* doing here?" Galahad asked, turning from the window and heading to the door.

"Same thing," Red said, stepping up to a roosting lark. "My mother likes updates." He gave Galahad a smile and pulled out a messenger tube.

Galahad smiled back weakly, and left. For some reason, he had the feeling he wasn't the only one who was hiding something.

CHAPTER 12

On the first day of quarantine, Calib didn't mind being stuck inside the council room so much. It was nice to have food delivered to them and to get out of chores. To pass the time, he, Devrin, and Warren continued to train with Kensington, working through techniques the commander had learned from her time as a traveling swordsmouse for hire.

"The step distracts your opponent, drawing their eyes away from your sword to your footpaws," Commander Kensington began, demonstrating an intricate maneuver on Devrin that involved sidestepping in the middle of an attack.

Devrin tried to anticipate Commander Kensington's next move, but she was a second too slow. Before Calib could blink, Kensington had brought the flat of her sword blade down on Devrin's tail. If Kensington hadn't turned her hilt at the last minute, the squire would have been short an inch of tail.

"And this is why they also call this move the Tail Chop," Kensington finished.

Watching them from her makeshift bed, Saffron sat up and smiled for the first time since she'd arrived. As they continued their practice, Warren and Calib began to add dialogue to entertain the squirrel-maiden.

"En garde, crumple-whiskers!" Warren said, referring to the fact that Calib's whiskers were often crooked. The gray mouse waved his sword dramatically. "Were you born with those or did lightning strike your face?"

"They're just shriveling at the sight of your ugly snout!" Calib teased back. Saffron laughed, and the sound made Calib happy—until she began to wheeze and gasp. Madame von Mandrake got up from her embroidering and calmed the squirrel with a chamomile sachet.

"Breathe into it, nice and slow," she whispered. Looking up at the rest of the group, she wagged a warning paw. "Quiet, Saffron needs rest."

The second day, there was no training, as Kensington decided peace and quiet were in order for Saffron's recovery. The group resorted to challenging one another with riddles.

"Why is it impossible to walk past an otter?" Devrin asked.

"Because there are no otter ways around it," Saffron chimed in. Out of all of them, the squirrel was the quickest with her answers.

Afterward, they exchanged stories. Madame shared a story about the time her inn was attacked by a sea witch. She claimed that only a protective elm charmed by a wizard had kept the witch's black magic at bay.

"In the morning," Madame said, "when the witch retreated, we all went outside. There was a patch of dead grass in the town courtyard across the street. The lovely elm tree that grew there had been burned black and was hard as a rock. People said lightning must have struck it, but we at the inn knew better."

Commander Kensington began to clap, and the others quickly joined in. "Well told, Viviana," Kensington said. "The coastal towns to the south are full of rich tales and legends. Port towns can't help but collect stories, with all its comings and goings."

"Isn't that where the stories of Avalon come from?" Saffron asked.

Kensington nodded. "A fool's quest for witless treasure hunters, no doubt."

"Well, I know what I experienced that night, and

it was not of this Earth," Madame von Mandrake said, straightening out her sash of herbs.

"It was a good story, Madame von Mandrake," Saffron said thoughtfully. "As good as the one the fortune-teller told us at the Spring Fair. She wore a wooden circlet on top of her hooded cloak. And if any creature touched it, the fortune-teller could catch a glimpse of the future."

Saffron looked down at her paws, and Calib saw two teardrops drip on them. "I guess if she were a true fortune-teller, she would have been able to warn us about the disease."

Calib's heart ached for Saffron. He too knew what it was like to have no more family to turn to. He held her too-hot paw, and she squeezed back gratefully.

"The days of Old Magic and wizardry are long gone from Britain," Commander Kensington said. "I prefer to deal with more straightforward matters."

"Say what you will, Commander," Madame said, "but I believe strange things still lurk in the far waters of our world."

On the third day, Saffron slept longer than usual. The worry in Madame's eyes grew deeper. The mouslings were told to sit in silence now. Calib wondered what Cecily and the others were doing. Probably playing out in the sun, with fresh air.

He must have made a face, because Madame gestured him over to the far corner and asked if he was feeling all right.

Calib decided to be truthful. "Cecily and I had a fight. I think she's still angry with me. . . ." His voice trailed off, uncertain of what to say. Madame patted his head.

"The first rule of healing is to focus on the cause, not the symptoms," she said kindly. "I know your heart, Calib. You want to be a hero and fix everything. But in this case, make sure that being the hero doesn't get in the way of the fixing."

Calib nodded but didn't follow. How could being a hero be a bad thing? Saffron and her village and maybe others as well were counting on them to find a cure. This was the *perfect* time to be a hero.

"I was thinking . . . Should we try to find Avalon?" Calib asked. "Whatever this disease is, we're not prepared for it. And it sounds like we could use some more healers at least."

Madame von Mandrake shook her head sadly. "I've thought about it as well, *chéri.* It's tempting, but we wouldn't even know where to begin. Avalon is not marked on any maps that we or the Two-Leggers possess, and we cannot spare any paws to chase a myth."

"Commander, how much longer will we be in quarantine?" Warren asked from across the room. Calib thought that Kensington would admonish Warren for breaking the quiet, but instead, she looked up from her reading toward the sleeping Saffron. Calib, following her gaze, saw that the squirrel's expression was troubled, like she was having nightmares.

Kensington turned to Warren. "Until we have answers."

CHAPTER 13

Galahad watched as Red moved fast and fluid around the training ring, parrying the strikes from Malcolm, one of the older pages, with ease and grace. The morning's combat practice had become less of a training and more of a demonstration. Passersby stopped what they were doing to observe while Galahad waited glumly for his turn.

"I hate to admit it, but Red's footwork is incredible," said the boy standing beside him.

Galahad scowled at Bors, the first friend he'd made at

Camelot. Bors was not easily impressed by anything that didn't have ancient writing scrawled across it. These days, he spent most of his time cataloging loose scrolls in the library. At the Battle of the Bear, an enemy arrow had struck Bors in his left knee, and the injury had left him with a limp. He'd remained at the castle, though, in order to learn and educate himself on scholarly pursuits.

"He's fine, I guess," Galahad said. "It's clear he's had training before he got here, which gives him an advantage."

Advantage was putting it lightly.

Red moved like a wildcat toying with his prey. Malcolm's signature move had always been to pin his opponents down to the ground as quickly as possible. Galahad had learned that the hard way last year. But Red was nimbly dodging his opponent's attempts to subdue him.

A murmur rose up behind Galahad. Turning, he saw that King Arthur and Sir Lancelot had entered the training courtyard. They were dressed for a hunt, but had stopped to observe the duel. As Red quickly leaped sideways to avoid another charge from Malcolm, he smacked the blade of his sword on Malcolm's back.

Everyone gasped.

"Excellent footwork, Red!" Lancelot commented.

Galahad felt a flair of jealousy come to his cheeks. Red's skill was undeniable. And there was no way Galahad could match it.

Red surged forward, stooping low and sweeping his feet to trip Malcolm. The bigger boy fell on his back with a thud. Red swung his wooden sword at Malcolm's neck, stopping short of contact. Red had moved with such speed, Galahad didn't even register what happened before thunderous applause rang out. No one seemed to be clapping harder than Sir Lancelot and King Arthur.

"You all right?" Red asked, offering a hand.

"I'm fine." Malcolm brushed off Red's hand, coughing and wheezing. He looked mad but also surprised. He was not used to losing.

Out of the corner of his eye, Galahad saw an out-of-breath servant run over to King Arthur. Eyes wide, he whispered something into the king's ears. Galahad watched the king's expression turn grim and pale. The king said something to Sir Lancelot, and the two of them returned to the castle. Galahad wondered what information had canceled their hunt, and worried that it might be the news he'd been dreading.

A jolt of unease sent a shiver down Galahad's spine. He had not heard anything from Calib for almost a week. Not since Galahad had given Calib and the tan mouse the medicine for their friend. Though the larks had not yet returned, Galahad had asked Father Walter to send for more feverfew supplies. Just in case.

He wondered where the birds had disappeared to, and

hoped nothing had happened to the animals. Suddenly, as though he'd conjured them with his thoughts, Galahad saw a small black speck over Bors's shoulder that looked like one of the birds as it drew nearer.

"I'm going for a quick jog around the arena to keep warmed up," Galahad said to Bors, hoping that this sounded like a genuine excuse. "If someone asks for me, say I'll be right back."

Galahad quickly ducked out and headed to the aviary.

"Finally!" he said as the lark landed on the ledge of a window, its tiny chest heaving. Galahad held his breath as he gently unbuttoned the bird's messenger pouch.

To his dismay, the pouch was empty. There was no message nor any new supplies. He frowned. What had snapped the twine from around the bird's leg? But his thoughts were interrupted by loud, urgent chirps.

The messenger lark perched on a stand, tweeting loudly to the others still in their cages.

Galahad slid his hand to his hilt. Apart from Calib, he'd rarely tried to communicate with any other animals, and even those attempts were always hit-or-miss. But he needed to try. He *had* to know what the bird had seen.

Taking a deep breath, Galahad focused all his will onto the messenger bird. He could feel the hilt of Excalibur grow warm in his palm, like a glow of energy.

To his astonishment, the chirping grew fainter as

feelings began to take shape in his head. Sensations of urgency and fear filled his mind like sharp, pecking stabs. Galahad concentrated even harder.

"Three villages in the west . . . A strange sickness! The man . . . so weak . . . couldn't even write. . . . I left as soon as I could!" the bird said to the others. "Tell Commander Kensington."

CHAPTER 14

On the seventh day of quarantine, the door to the council room creaked open. Calib perked up his ears. Sir Alric's red eyes peered around the corner.

"Alric, what part of 'quarantine' don't you understand?" Commander Kensington roared as she surged up from her seat.

But Sir Alric only shook his head. "I'm afraid it's too late for that."

A knot twisted in Calib's stomach as the white mouse opened the door wider to let in a bell-tower lark and one of Calib's favorite bird friends, Valentina Stormbeak, a scouting crow of the Darkling Woods.

"Ranger Stormbeak and General Fletcher," Commander Kensington said, "what is the meaning of this?"

The lark hopped forward and saluted with his wing. "I was sent by a Two-Legger to find out about sickness in the land. . . ."

"How did a Two-Legger know to ask such a question?" Kensington demanded. Calib looked down at his footpaws. He knew very well who the Two-Legger must have been, but he wasn't going to say anything. When the lark could only shrug, Kensington waved him on impatiently.

The bird took two more nervous hops. "All the villages I found were laid low with fever. Two-Leggers and creatures both."

Calib's paws began to tremble.

"There's more," Valentina added grimly. "The crow patrols have seen the same thing, and scores of them are sick now. A few of the castle orchard mice are also ill, as are some of Arthur's human servants. There is no longer need for quarantine. The sickness is already among us."

A stricken silence followed. Calib found himself holding his breath, as if the very air was already poisoned. He wondered if this was how it began the last time the sea fever swept through their land: with a breath and the cold certainty that this foe could not be defeated with a sword.

"I'm sorry!" Saffron's mumbled softly. "This is all my fault."

"You alone could not have spread it so quickly," Commander Kensington reassured her. "Something else is at work."

The mouse-leader addressed everyone gathered. "You are all dismissed to go back to your daily duties. Saffron, we should move you to a proper bed."

The commander looked over at Madame von Mandrake. "Let's put her in Yvers's old room. In the meantime, we monitor everyone for headaches or fevers."

Calib's stomach was already feeling queasy. The quarantine was lifted, but no one felt reassured.

Warren and Calib made their way back to the boys' dorms to wash up, following the path of support beams that crisscrossed the Two-Legger sleeping quarters. Rumors were being shared in hushed tones from Two-Legger to Two-Legger below. Calib paused to listen but could only catch bits and pieces.

"The entire kitchen staff . . . It acts so quickly. . . ."

"I have a headache; do you think . . . Could it be?" As they walked, Calib noticed other mice gave them extra space. Their eyes followed them as they passed.

"I wish they'd stop staring," Calib muttered to Warren.

"I'm just glad I don't have to spend another night sleeping under the table," the gray mouse replied. "I miss my sock." Warren *did* look more exhausted than usual.

Calib picked up the pace, wishing he was already in the security of the snug dorm, away from everyone's suspicious eyes.

But when he and Warren opened the door, there was something else. Or rather, *someone* else.

"Hey, no girls in the boys' room!" Warren said wearily.

Dandelion looked up with fearful tears in her eyes. "I'm s-s-sorry. He was t-t-too afraid to tell anyone. I've been trying to take care of him, but I'm—I'm just no good at it!" she whispered, whiskers drooping to her chin.

Calib's heart squeezed. Though he could hardly hear what Dandelion was saying, he thought he understood. Fearfully, he drew back the covers.

Young Edwin lay in his bed, curled up into a tiny ball and shivering with fever.

CHAPTER 15

"This is not good."

Father Walter squinted at an empty amber bottle. "Mudberry can be a dangerous poison in untrained hands. And with the feverfew gone . . ."

The first word of the village sicknesses had reached the castle, and now much of the kitchen staff had succumbed to headaches. Father Walter, even with his extensive knowledge, did not know how to treat it. At first, the healer thought it was sea fever, but he had quickly changed his diagnosis. The sea fever was usually accompanied by a rash, while this sickness struck with little warning. It was something new and unknown.

"I'm sorry," Galahad said miserably. "None of the villages responded to me when I asked for more." He had finished up his afternoon supply tally, but some items were not adding up. The feverfew blossoms and now the mudberry supplies were both missing.

"I'll ask if the town herbalist saved any from last year," the old man said with a sigh. He set out a cutting board and pulled a small knife from his workbench. "Feverfew isn't due to bloom for another few weeks yet."

Galahad nodded, feeling a little guilty for giving away so much to the mice. "How can I help?"

"I suggest you go to the library and look through Merlin's Scrolls." Father Walter began chopping ginger. "Perhaps Merlin foretold this in his vast prophecies and writings."

Surprised, Galahad looked away from the empty shelves and toward Father Walter. "I thought you said magic was a bunch of nonsense."

Merlin's sudden disappearance ten years ago was the subject of much debate at Camelot. Some thought he'd left, traveled beyond the Sapphire Sea to wilds unknown. But others suspected foul play. The wizard had gained some enemies in his time in King Arthur's court. Some thought he was a charlatan with too much power or that his magic was a lie. Others thought he had lost his touch with his advancing age.

Then one day, when Arthur called upon Merlin to advise him on his final attack against the Saxons, they discovered that Merlin was missing and his chambers empty, except for a mountain of written scrolls.

"I never put faith in magic," the healer replied as he shook an envelope above his worktable. A few pitiful leaves drifted out. "I prefer to deal in things I can see and what can be proven."

With a sigh, Walter set the envelope down and reached for his satchel. He looked sentimental as he swung it over his hunched shoulder. "But I believed in the man who called himself Merlin—there was greatness and power there. Would I call it magic? I don't know. But perhaps wisdom is its own form of magic."

"What should I be looking for?" Galahad asked. "They say half of Merlin's Scrolls are written in code."

"I believe Merlin's intention was that the answers would reveal themselves only at the right time to the right person," Father Walter said.

"But why me?" The question slipped out before Galahad could stop it. It had been waiting so long to be asked, had nudged and poked and prodded every night since the events of last fall unfolded. He'd pushed it back, not wanting to let others know that he was just as confused as they were.

"Because," Father Walter said gently, "you ask the right questions."

CHAPTER 16

At first, Calib thought only Edwin would fall ill within the walls, but he was wrong. Word soon came that the fever had struck some of the larks. Then the hedgehog mead brewers. The mole archivists. The vole blacksmiths.

And then one day, as Calib searched for feverfew with Madame von Mandrake and the other pages in the Darkling Woods, there was a sudden cry. Turning back, they saw Barnaby propping up Warren.

"I don't know what happened," Barnaby said. "He just kind of . . . flopped."

"Just a dizzy spell, that's all," the gray mouse replied woozily.

Madame von Mandrake rushed over and placed a paw against Warren's forehead. "You're running a fever," she said, tsking. "You should have said you were feeling ill!" She motioned to the rest of the pages. "Help him get back to the infirmary with the others."

With an arm under each shoulder, Barnaby and Devrin lifted Warren to his footpaws.

"I—I was hoping it would go away," Warren mumbled. "I'm sorry."

Warren Clipping hardly ever apologized for anything. Even though he could be a spoiled brat sometimes, Calib's heart ached at the sight of him slumped over like a rag doll.

As they neared the drawbridge, a kitchen mouse ran out to meet them. A white pawkerchief was wrapped around her snout like a mask.

"Oh, thank Merlin!" she panted. "Madame von Mandrake, you must come quickly!"

"What's the matter?"

"It's Saffron! We thought she was getting better—her fever has been low all day—but when I brought her lunch just now, she wouldn't wake up to eat it!"

"Dandelion and Barnaby, take Warren. I'll be there shortly. The rest of you, come with me."

Madame von Mandrake broke into a run, the bag of feverfew blossoms slung over her shoulder. Forgetting the rip in her bag, she didn't notice the feverfew petals falling behind her in a trail of white, with Calib, Cecily, and Devrin following close behind.

They entered Yvers's room, where Saffron had been moved after the quarantine had been lifted. Commander Kensington had never found it in her heart to get rid of Yvers's old things so that she could take over his chambers, and had decided to keep her own separate quarters instead. Calib's heart caught in his throat as he stepped in. He had not been in since his grandfather's funeral.

Saffron lay in a canopy bed, buried under many blankets. Her tufted ears lay flat against her head, and her eyes were closed. Only the slightest rise and fall of her chest reassured Calib that the worst had not happened yet.

The commander, in a dark-purple cloak, hovered by the bedside. Sir Alric perched on the mattress, holding a small, hornlike instrument to Saffron's chest.

"Her pulse is weak," Sir Alric squeaked after listening for a few seconds. He shook his head. "And her fever has gotten worse."

"I've brought the feverfew we collected," Madame von Mandrake said. "Let's brew it quickly. Calib, could you help?"

Calib scooped a pawful of the feverfew leaves and

dumped them into a teakettle that hung in the fireplace. His attention fell on a finely made mouse-sized broadsword that was displayed over the mantel. It was his father's, Sir Trenton's, sword, Darkslayer. The sight of it gave him small courage. What would his father do in a situation like this?

As the tea began to brew, a bitter, lemony scent wafted into the air. After blowing on the feverfew to cool it, Madame Von Mandrake gently poured a small amount down Saffron's throat.

The squirrel came to with a start. "Wh . . . what?" she muttered weakly. "Mama?" A dry cough heaved its way out of her, and Calib's own rib cage seemed to tighten with the sound.

"She's awake," Madame said breathlessly. "Thank Merlin!"

"I dreamed I was with my family again," Saffron said, her voice barely a scrape. "They were beckoning me in the Fields Beyond."

"Viviana!" A shrew nurse hurried into the room, panting heavily. "We need more help in the infirmary. Creatures from the Darkling Woods are coming in seeking aid." She clutched a stitch in her side, clearly having run to Yvers's chambers with her news. "The otters wish to speak with you, Commander Kensington. They request to be relieved of their sentry duties, as too many of them have fallen sick."

"I'll be there shortly," Kensington said. She closed her eyes for a moment, as if a great weariness had come over her. "Sir Alric, please accompany Madame von Mandrake. Devrin, you will be in charge of the sentries from here on out. Please find some pages to relieve the otters."

Devrin's wide eyes echoed Calib's surprise: were they already that low on soldiers? Nevertheless, she saluted. "Yes, Commander."

Madame von Mandrake stood and grabbed the bag of feverfew, preparing to leave. "Someone should stay with her," she said, nodding at Saffron. "Make sure she drinks her tea."

"I can," Calib said. He pulled up a stool next to the bed and cradled the cup in his paws. Saffron seemed so small curled on her pillows. Smaller even than that day he'd helped pull her from the river.

After the others left the room, Calib gently held the teacup to Saffron's mouth until she swallowed a few sips. A determination gripped him. He hadn't saved Saffron from the waterfalls only for her to get sicker. He'd do everything he could to make sure she saw another Spring Fair in her village.

"Stay awake, Saffron," he pleaded. "I'll tell you stories."

And though she didn't say anything, Calib thought he saw her face relax. He recounted all the tall tales and myths he knew from memory, including some of his grandfather's and father's legendary feats. He even told the funnier tales, like how his grandfather had once lit the commander's cloak on fire when he was a page. After four more stories, Saffron had finished nearly all of her tea.

"Thank you," she said, her head denting the pillow. "I feel . . . well, not good, but better."

"I'll get some more," Calib said. He stood up and walked to the fireplace. As before, his eyes were drawn to his father's beautiful sword gleaming over the fireplace mantel.

"The thin places . . ."

Calib turned. Saffron was still awake, but her eyes had a faraway look.

"What was that?" he asked.

In her feverish state, she began to sing:

"The thin places of the land are three,
Two by stone, one by sea."

Calib quickly refilled the teacup. She had seemed well only a moment before. . . .

"Avalon . . . Promise me," she said, when Calib brought the final cup of feverfew tea over. She squinted as if she was having a hard time focusing. "Promise me that you'll go to Avalon. Do what I could not."

Calib paused, uncertain. Saffron wasn't making any

sense. And Madame von Madrake was right—they didn't even know where to start to find the mysterious island.

"I promise that when you get better, we can ask Commander Kensington to send some knights on the mission," Calib said brightly, hoping that the answer would be good enough.

"No!" The squirrel's head tossed back and forth. "Promise me you'll go to the thin places. It'll help me sleep better."

Her paw clasped over Calib's. The pads were dry, hot to the touch. "Promise!"

"I—I promise I'll do my best to find a cure," Calib said.

"Go to Avalon," Saffron repeated.

His insides squirmed, but finally, he gave in. "I promise to go to Avalon."

"Thank you," Saffron said, releasing his paw. "You're a good friend." She nestled her head deeper into the pillow, looking more peaceful than she had in days.

Calib began to talk again, until his own eyelids began to droop. It was only when the teacup slipped out of his paw and broke on the floor that he realized he had fallen asleep. The fire had burned down to embers, and the room had grown chilly. He rubbed the sleep from his eyes.

"Do you want more tea?" Calib shook her shoulder. "Saffron?"

The squirrel did not stir. Her eyes were shut, and her expression peaceful, but her paw felt cold. She lay as still as a statue.

Calib stumbled back, upsetting the stool he had been sitting on. He sprinted out into the hall to seek help. "Madame von Mandrake! Commander! Somebody come quick! *Oof!*"

He had run headlong into Cecily.

"Ceci— It's Saffron!" he all but yelled. "She's— What's wrong?" He'd suddenly noticed the tears that were coursing down Cecily's cheeks and onto her pink nose.

"Maman . . . she's sick," Cecily choked out. "And Warren's fever won't go down. The fever is taking everyone!"

Their fight forgotten, Calib pulled Cecily into a tight hug, as if it might form some sense of armor against death.

CHAPTER 17

Galahad snapped the book shut, and the old, tired pages sent out a puff a dust.

"There's no mention of a sickness in here either," he said irritably. "Or if there is, I didn't translate it correctly. I'm not sure it's even written in Latin."

Bors peered over his shoulder and looked down at one of several hundreds of records that held Merlin's writing. "'*Numquam ericium iratum amplectere,*'" Bors read aloud. He shrugged. "You haven't been practicing. The sentence is clear to me: 'never hug an angry hedgehog.'"

Baffled, Galahad stared down at the spidery writing on the cover. "Why would I?" he asked. "I wouldn't even hug a happy one." Laying his head on the desk, he let out a long sigh. "None of this is what we're looking for."

"I'm not sure what we *are* supposed to be looking for," Bors said, rubbing his bleary eyes. "Most of it is gobbledygook with silly sentences like this. I think there must be some truth about Merlin going funny in his old age."

Galahad pulled another tome and opened it. Strangely, it was mostly blank with only a few runes scrawled at the top of some pages: the sun, the moon, what looked to be a cup. He reached for another book.

"Just follow the dates and see if you find anything that has the word 'sickness' or 'disease,'" he said. "Father Walter said that near the end, Merlin spent most of his time scrying to see Camelot's fate. Maybe he saw Sir Kay trying to catch a hedgehog or something."

Bors let out a tired chuckle and returned to reading. Galahad tried to do the same. At the beginning of his search, he had been optimistic. He'd even fantasized once or twice about the moment he would find the cure, clear as day on the page, and present it to King Arthur. He would be hailed as the hero of Camelot again, and Red would just be an afterthought.

But after hours of scouring, Galahad had recruited Bors, who'd done best in their Latin studies, to help him decipher some of Merlin's extensive writings. The stacks of scrolls and books took up nearly half the library.

The two were huddled around a single candle, trying to read discreetly without setting any of the delicate pages on fire. Merlin was prolific; the wizard wrote everything down, from the day-to-day happenings of castle life to his strangest dreams and visions.

"What are you two up to in here?"

Red's head popped around the shelf, startling them. He seemed to have just come up from supper, judging by the dinner roll in his hand. It was slightly burned, since in the absence of the cooks, all meals were being prepared by Guinevere's ladies-in-waiting and the younger squires, who had no great familiarity with being in a kitchen.

"We're trying to see if Merlin left any clues about this sickness," Bors said before Galahad had chance to kick him under the table.

Galahad shot Bors a glare. If word got out that there was no cure—that this was not the sea fever but something else—panic would ensue.

And though he was slightly ashamed to admit it even to himself, *he* wanted to be the one to find the cure. If he did, maybe his father, the greatest knight Camelot had ever seen, wouldn't be so mad that his son wanted to become a common healer.

"Merlin's Scrolls?" Red asked. "I didn't realize they'd

keep them out in the open like this. I thought they would have been better hidden, maybe in a secret cave or something."

Galahad hunched over his current book. "Merlin dedicated his life to Camelot," he said. "He wouldn't want his work locked up and seen by only a few. He'd want everyone to have access to it."

Red picked up the book Galahad had set aside and read a few pieces out loud in perfect Latin. Galahad fought hard to keep his eyes from rolling. Of course Red would be good at Latin *and* fighting.

"Careful that you don't say something that will spell you into a snake," Galahad said, trying to keep his voice light.

"I know what I'm doing," Red said nonchalantly. "Languages run in the family. My mother could communicate with forty different species of snake."

"That's . . . good for her, I guess?" Bors said, sounding perplexed at Red's serious response to Galahad's joke.

"Has reading these scrolls given you any insight to your magical sword?" Red asked, turning to Galahad.

"No," Galahad responded uneasily. Red took more interest in Excalibur than Galahad felt comfortable with. This was the second time this week he'd brought it up in conversation. "Why would it?"

Red cocked an eyebrow. "Don't you know about

Merlin's role with the first Sword in the Stone?"

Silence.

Galahad's face felt suddenly hot as even Bors looked back at him with an expectant look.

"No, I don't," Galahad gritted out. "I wasn't taught about Merlin at St. Anne's."

Red smiled knowingly, like a tutor relishing his lecture. "Sources say Merlin and the Sword in the Stone are connected by powerful magic. The wizard actually found Arthur after dreaming about a great king who would bring everlasting peace to Britain," Red said.

A small doubt sprouted in Galahad's mind. No great authority like Merlin had brought him to Excalibur. In fact, all he did was follow the instructions of a small mouse. Could it be that the sword wasn't meant for him but for a greater hero, someone more accomplished, like Red?

"I assume that was how you were led to the Sword, too, Galahad," Red continued. "By Merlin?"

Galahad closed his book. He'd had enough of Red's prying. "If it was, I wouldn't be at liberty to tell you."

"No need to get testy." Red raised his hands in mock defense. "Just trying to offer my help."

"I think we're doing quite well on our own," Bors said, sensing his friend's distress.

"I know many things. A wizard is only as good as

his secrets." Red shrugged as he left the library. "Could save you a lot of trouble later."

As Red's auburn head out the door, Galahad puzzled over what he'd said. Even hours later, he still couldn't tell if it was meant to be advice . . . or a threat.

CHAPTER 18

Saffron's funeral was a simple and quiet affair. They gathered on the riverbank, near the exact spot where Calib had first spied the squirrel's boat. That same boat would now carry her body to the Fields Beyond.

One by one, the creatures of Camelot lined up to pay their last respects and lay a flower in the boat. Calib joined Cecily at the end of line. They greeted each other silently. Calib could see that she had not slept either.

At last, it was Calib's turn. Trembling, he felt as if he were in a tournament challenge again, afraid to move a hair.

He felt Cecily's paw slip into his.

"How about we do it together?" she whispered. Calib nodded gratefully, and paw in paw, they walked together to the longboat. Saffron's body lay on a small pyre at the boat's center, a mirror image of how she had first arrived at Camelot.

"We will find a cure, I promise. I will find Avalon," Calib whispered, laying a small pea blossom in the boat before rejoining the others clustered on the shore.

Dandelion cleared her throat. With no musical accompaniment, she began to sing a sorrowful melody that made Calib's heart swell.

"Fare thee well, dear traveler,
Down that far and winding road.
At end of paths, at end of days,
You will lay down a heavy load."

Dandelion's last note drifted off into silence. The chapel bells began to toll with sweeping and hollow peals, echoing far into the surrounding hills.

Bo-ong!

Kensington untied the twine that anchored the boat to shore. Slowly, the reed boat drifted away from them, bearing its treasured cargo toward the waterfalls.

Bo-ong!

As it floated into the stronger currents, Macie Cornwall stepped forward with her bow. Dipping the tip of an arrow into a nearby brazier, she lit the cloth arrowhead on fire.

Bo-ong!

Macie aimed at the boat and let loose the flaming arrow. It arced across the river like a comet and landed in the boat as it traveled down the river. Within moments, flames were licking the hull of the vessel. A thick column of smoke rose into the sky and fanned out over the moat like a ghostly spirit.

After the funeral, Calib, Cecily, Barnaby, and Dandelion sat together at breakfast, silently choking down their cold oatmeal. Training was suspended for the time being. And with Madame von Mandrake out of the kitchen, the food just did not taste as it should.

"I can't do this anymore," Cecily said, slamming her spoon down and sending specks of oatmeal flying.

"It's not your mother's cooking, I agree," Barnaby said, his mouth full. "But it's edible with some cinnamon."

"No, not the food—this!" she shouted, gesturing around at all of them. There was a wild determination in her eyes. "This waiting around for the disease to get us! We don't even *know* if it's sea fever. None of the normal remedies have had any effect. The cure will not be found at Camelot, no matter how many feverfew blossoms we collect."

"Then where do you suggest we look?" Barnaby asked.

"Avalon," Calib said quietly. "Last night, Saffron sang

a song, something about thin places. . . ."

But the last day had held so much sorrow and change that he couldn't remember the melody. He furrowed his brow, trying to remember. "'The thin places of the land are three. Two by stone, one by sea.'"

"Avalon, Avebury, and Amesbury," Dandelion finished the song meekly into her cold oatmeal.

"What's that?" Cecily asked, her ears perked.

"It's just an old shanty I picked up when our clan lived closer to the sea." Dandelion shrugged. "It doesn't even make any sense."

"Do you remember the rest?" Calib asked, his heart beating a little faster. This was the first real clue they'd come across.

"Of course. I've memorized all the sea shanties. This one was called 'Merlin's Call.'" She cleared her throat. In a clear voice, she began to sing:

"The thin places of the land are three
Two by stone, one by sea,
Avalon, Avebury, and Amesbury.
The ley lines line them equally
In a shape with faces three,
But I'll tell you which I'd rather see;
The dead won't talk, the fairies flee;
Stone can do nary harm to thee.

But in the depths of the blackest sea,
Avalon's beast may look back at me.
And when it eyes your company
Only Avalon's mark will let you be.
The one who bears it sets you free."

"I've never heard of these places," Barnaby said, reaching for the jam.

"Avebury and Amesbury are about a day's ride on horse from here," Cecily said. Her tail whipped back and forth in excitement. "They're said to be fairy hills—some of the few places Old Magic still seeps into our world."

"So it's a riddle, then," Calib said, his paws trembling. "Those must be what the 'two by stone' lines refer to."

"But what about Avalon's beast?" Barnaby asked. "That doesn't sound very nice." He scooped more oatmeal into his mouth.

"We can ask the Two-Leggers," Calib suggested.

Barnaby frowned. "Ash the oo-'eggers?" He swallowed. "Ask the Two-Leggers? What do you mean?"

"I meant," Calib said hastily, "the Two-Legger library. We should look there before we leave."

He felt a small tap on his pawfoot. Glancing across the table, he saw Cecily smile for the first time in days. It felt like a ray of sunshine on Calib's insides. He felt a little less helpless, and that meant everything.

"Could I come along too?" Barnaby asked. "I don't want to miss out on the next adventure. Like Sir Alric said, I need to discover my qualities." Barnaby had only lasted one week as the engineer's apprentice. Sir Alric didn't want him in his workshop after he accidentally caught his own tail in a mousetrap.

"Me too! I want to come too!" Dandelion implored.

Calib and Cecily looked at each other. Calib couldn't risk letting both of them in on the secret about Galahad. Cecily seemed to understand.

She shook her head. "Sorry, but we'll need our fastest runners on this mission."

"But if I don't get out of this castle, how will I figure out what my calling is?" Barnaby insisted, his whiskers drooping.

"And I know all about the woods!" Dandelion said, crossing her arms.

Cecily tried a gentler approach. "Kensington will need a lot of help in the next few days. And you two are some of our best helpers."

Barnaby nodded, but he still looked glum, and he continued to look glum even after they had finished breakfast. It wasn't until Cecily mentioned that the first spring strawberries were out that he cheered up. He and Dandelion went to look for more feverfew (and, Calib suspected, strawberries) while Calib and Cecily went to find Galahad.

They made their way out of the dining hall, following a series of tunnels running underneath the floorboards. But Calib noticed something had changed in the way the castle sounded.

He twitched his whiskers and strained his ears, but there was no creaking of feet above them. Odd.

Usually, there was a constant thrum of footsteps and Two-Legger chatter after breakfast—knights making their way to the training fields, craftsmen to the markets. Yet, the halls of Camelot were eerily quiet.

Curious, the two mice climbed onto a nearby windowsill. They peeked out onto one of the main thoroughfares in the courtyard and found it completely abandoned. No farmers bringing in fruits from the gardens. No mouth-watering smells of food wafting from the kitchen.

"Where *is* everyone?" Calib asked.

"I . . . I think they're all ill," Cecily said in a hushed voice.

They quickened their pace.

CHAPTER 19

They found Galahad in the library. The boy was fast asleep at a desk, using an opened book as a pillow. There were darkened rings under the boy's eyes, and his skin was pale. Calib's heart beat quickly. He didn't know what they would do if Galahad was also sick.

Calib sprinted down the rafters, with Cecily close behind, then climbed onto Galahad's chest. He laid a firm paw on Galahad's chin and shook.

Galahad's eyes fluttered awake. "I was wondering when I might see you again," he mumbled, fingers brushing the sword hilt he kept strapped to his side, even as he slept.

"Are you sick?" Calib asked immediately. He pantomimed fainting and pointed to the boy.

"No," Galahad said. "I've just been staying up late, reading."

"Thank Merlin!" Calib sighed.

Calib and Galahad exchanged stories, catching each other up on all that had happened, from the dwindling supply of feverfew to the castle's newest guest, King Arthur's nephew. Some of it required some paw waving and acting as Galahad struggled to understand a few mouse terms. But for the most part, the Two-Legger seemed to be growing stronger with his skill for hearing. Cecily looked back and forth, still in obvious awe that the conversation could happen at all.

"We're just as lost as you are," Galahad said. "The king and queen have been confined to their quarters for safety. And no one is allowed to stand within five feet of one another, or leave the castle."

"We have an idea," Calib said. "We think we can find a cure. But we need to get to Avalon."

Galahad looked confused. "Avalon? I thought the island was just a rumor told by land-starved sailors."

Calib relayed the sea shanty to him. When he'd finished, he added, "We think it's a clue on how to get there."

After a moment's thinking, the boy held out his palm for Calib and Cecily to climb onboard. "Let's go to the cartographer's archives.'"

"Not the pocket again!" Cecily squeaked.

Galahad's hand stopped. "I'm sorry it's so uncomfortable," he said apologetically. "It'll just be a moment."

Calib expected Cecily to protest more, but whether it was the promise of a short trip or the fact that Cecily was so surprised at Galahad addressing her, she nodded mutely. Calib caught himself smiling at Cecily's nervousness. He didn't think there was much that could fluster her.

After a bumpy ride across the library and up a flight of stairs, they were in the cartographer's archives. There, Galahad pulled out a large map of Britain and unrolled it over a chessboard.

"First, let's mark where Avebury and Amesbury are," Cecily said, rolling a rook over to where Stonehenge was. Calib followed her lead and pushed a knight over to Avebury.

"'The ley lines line them equally,'" Galahad repeated the lyric as he drew a straight line from Avebury to Amesbury.

"What are ley lines?" Calib asked.

Galahad's eyes brightened. "I just learned this from Merlin's Scrolls. They say the first settlers of Britain built prayer circles based on mystical lines that run through our land. If the song is hinting that Avalon is equal distance from these two points . . ."

"'The ley lines *line them equally,*'" Cecily echoed.

"Right." Galahad then drew two more lines that met at a point northwest of Avebury and Amesbury, forming a triangle, and then another set of lines that met at a point southeast of the circles. "Then it could be here or here." Galahad pointed to the tops of the triangles he had drawn.

The northern point ended in a lake, not too far from them. The other was in the Emerald Sea, far south. Calib paced the map, crossing huge distances with each step.

"Which direction makes the most sense?" Galahad rubbed his temples.

"I know which one looks easiest," Cecily said, footpaw tapping on the lake.

Calib looked down at his own footpaws. He'd stopped pacing at the compass rose. The artist had painted a mermaid around it or, perhaps, a sea witch, whose hair curled around his toes. It reminded him of Madame von Mandrake's story and how the origins of the Avalon legend originated from the south . . . from along the Emerald Sea. An idea stirred.

"Cecily, where did you say you and your mother are from?"

Cecily's eyes widened, and she pointed to a town very close to the southeastern point. "The port town of

Poole—known mostly for its pastries; treasure hunters; and stories of magic, myth, and lore."

Perhaps there was a clue hidden in Madame von Mandrake's story about the sea witch. If magic like that still existed in the world, it must be from Avalon.

"Then that decides it," Calib said, feeling resolve circling his heart and pulling tight. "We go south."

"I'll saddle my horse," Galahad said. Though there were still purple circles beneath his eyes, life seemed to have come back to his cheeks. Calib felt the same way—the very *possibility* that they could *do* something banished his own exhaustion.

But even as Calib looked at Galahad, he saw something shift within the Two-Legger, and the weariness settled back over him.

"I will make sure you two get safe passage out of the castle," Galahad said quietly. "There are ways around the quarantine."

Calib's ears swiveled toward the Two-Legger in surprise. "You don't want to come with us?"

"I do," Galahad said, and Calib heard the aching timber that told him the boy was telling the truth. "But . . . there aren't enough healers in the castle. If more fall ill, or if Father Walter does, then there's no one who could help."

Calib tried not to let his whiskers droop. He didn't want to make Galahad feel more miserable than he already did. They would have covered ground so much quicker with Two-Legger aid.

"That's all right," Calib said. "We can manage on our own."

"And"—Cecily prodded him in the ribs—"there still might be answers in Merlin's Scrolls. He shouldn't give up! We *can't* give up." Cecily's voice broke. "Too many depend on finding the answers."

Calib squeezed his friend's paw. Galahad nodded.

"I have an idea for how to get you there faster, at least," the boy said, patting Calib gently on his shoulder with a finger. "I just need to speak with my friend."

Cecily sniffled while Calib nodded, his eyes putting the map to memory. Somewhere near the southeast corner of the kingdom lay Avalon, and their best chance to find a cure.

CHAPTER 20

Later that evening, Calib rummaged in the Two-Legger cellars, packing for their secret journey. At dawn, they would leave. He was supposed to be tending to Warren, but the gray mouse would have none of it.

"I'd rather pluck my whiskers than let you spoon-feed me," he said. Even at his weakest, Warren still had a few wisecracks in him. "Go on, then, find Avalon. I'll manage on my own."

Aided by a single small candle, Calib walked the shadowy corridors, breathing in smells of musty cheese, dry grain, and jerky. Spotting an open barrel of dried anchovies, Calib stopped to shove some loose fish into his backpack.

He tested its weight. To make sure the sack would not constrain him in a fight, he practiced a few moves using an anchovy as his sword.

"En garde!" The fish head fell off and rolled into the darkness.

He looked at the headless anchovy in his paw and felt sheepish. Calib didn't even have a proper weapon yet. Cecily at least had kept hers from their adventures last fall.

He remembered his father's sword hanging in Commander Yvers's room, its blade shining and itching to be used. Surely his grandfather had meant to give it to him when he was ready. What better time than now, right before he was to embark on another quest? The sword was his birthright, and he couldn't wait around for someone to give it to him. He had to claim it, as any hero would do.

Calib decided to go to Yvers's room. Climbing up the stairwell from the cellars to the Two-Legger kitchens, Calib was once again struck by how eerily quiet Camelot had become. He almost missed the sounds of cooks yelling, even if they were chasing mice out of the kitchen.

Suddenly, he heard a sound of something falling, followed by a curse. Thinking someone was in trouble, Calib followed the direction of the noise to the Two-Legger library.

Curious, the mouse ventured into the rows of musty-smelling scrolls and tomes. He rounded the corner slowly and hid behind a loose copy of an illuminated prayer book.

A few feet away stood a Two-Legger boy whom Calib did not recognize. His reddish hair obscured his features as he hunched over an open scroll. A small pile was already stacked at his feet.

An uneasy feeling prickled Calib. It was strange to be reading so late. For a moment, he was tempted to stay and watch, but the urgency of his current mission outweighed his curiosity. The mouse scampered past to get to the main dorms.

Calib held his breath as he tiptoed into Yvers's room. He hadn't been inside his grandfather's chambers since Saffron had died. And even though he knew it was just superstition, part of him felt that Saffron's spirit must still linger here, waiting for Calib to fulfill his promise to her. The thought spooked him, and he hurried to the fireplace.

But his father's sword, Darkslayer, no longer hung there.

Perturbed, Calib riffled through the trunks and chests, but turned up no sign of the legendary blade. Instead, his paws grazed across a velvet-lined robe embroidered with the Christopher crest.

His grandfather had lived simply, always donating gifts back to the poor of Camelot. His only luxury had been his fine ceremonial robes. Calib stroked the velvet, a lump as large as a pea forming in his throat. What he wouldn't give to have one more hour—one more *minute*—with his grandfather.

The hinges of the door creaked, as if in reply. Stories of ghosts and ghouls rushed into his mind again.

"Grandfather, is that you?" Calib whispered tentatively. "Saffron?"

Just as he was about to place a paw on the bedroom door, it swung open from the other side. The sharp eyes of Commander Kensington glared imperiously down at him.

"Calib Christopher," the commander said, stepping out to place a strong paw on his shoulder. "I was concerned. I had come to the infirmary to give you something, but Warren insisted that you had gone to bed early. How are you feeling?"

"No headache yet, Commander, if that's what you're wondering," Calib said.

"That is good, but what are you doing here?"

Calib tried to keep his face blank. If Kensington knew what he was truly up to, she'd forbid it. "I'm just so tired, and Barnaby snores loudly. I thought I could sleep here. . . ."

Commander Kensington narrowed her eyes. "Is that so? Are you sure you weren't looking for this?" From behind her back, she produced Sir Trenton's broadsword.

She unsheathed Darkslayer; the shining silver blade slipping out soundlessly. It was the finest thing Calib had ever seen. The handle, shaped with a mouse's grip in mind, was wrapped in dark-red leather. The Christopher crest, a goblet with rays of sunlight shooting upward from it, was embossed on the pommel.

Calib trembled from whisker tip to tail.

Commander Kensington smiled at Calib. "I think Yvers was saving this for the day you were to be knighted," she said. In a fluid, swift motion, she slid it back into the scabbard. She held the handle out to Calib. "But need trumps tradition in this case, I think."

Calib felt rooted to the spot where he stood, overcome with disbelief and elation. With a tentative paw, he took the sword from Commander Kensington. It felt lighter than it looked, masterful work on the part of the swordsmith. Cradling the other end with the crook of his elbow, Calib held the sword close to his pounding heart. He struggled for the right words to say. "Thank you" didn't even come close.

"One last word of advice," Kensington said as she slipped toward the door. "Dried fish gives off a strong scent. Stick to nuts and berries and bring a fishing rod instead."

Calib looked at her, dumbfounded. "I'm not sure what you mean, Commander. . . ."

Kensington paused before a portrait of one of Calib's ancestors, a mouse with crooked whiskers. She studied it, paw on chin, while she mused aloud. "I've decreed that no one is allowed to leave the boundaries of this castle. If the commander knew of such a plot or quest to sneak out and seek a cure, she'd have to forbid it. But if she did not know of such a plot, she couldn't forbid it, could she?"

Understanding dawned on Calib. "No, she couldn't, Commander."

"So in your interest," Kensington said, taking a step away from the painting and staring hard at Calib, "I believe you heard me loud and clear."

He saluted as hard as he could. Commander Kensington nodded and walked out of Yvers's room. Calib slipped out after her, the beating of his heart a war drum in his ears.

CHAPTER 21

The castle gate groaned like a waking giant, and the chains rattled as the drawbridge lowered across Camelot's moat. Calib and Cecily braced themselves against a corner of the medicine box.

"Could we not wake up the entire castle, Bors?" Calib could hear Galahad's worried voice filter through the cracks in the wooden box—the one that was filled with empty vials and two questing mice.

Everything jostled as Galahad handed over the box to Bors. "Do I have to remind you that what we're doing is supposed to be a secret?"

"This is as quiet as I can make a castle gate," Bors said. The box shifted again as it was set into a saddlebag.

"Sorry," Calib said as he bumped into Cecily. She nodded a silent acceptance and helped push him back onto his feet.

"If we're caught outside of quarantine, we'll be in big trouble," Galahad whispered.

"Only if there's anyone *left* to punish us," Bors retorted.

A strangled sound came from Cecily, and Calib saw that her nose had gone pale. Calib narrowed his eyes. If it wasn't important that he and Cecily remained a secret, he would have jabbed Darkslayer between Bors's toes. There was no need to be so insensitive!

"Bors!" Galahad admonished.

"You know I don't mean it," Bors said hurriedly. "It's just . . . well . . . hard, not knowing what's going to happen, you know? I'm only laughing in the dark."

"I know," Galahad said gently. "You have the list of things you need to get?"

"Yes, though I don't know why I need to go all the way to Poole for it."

"None of the villages have responded to our resupply requests. We'll have to travel farther afield, where we don't have regular contact," Galahad replied, his voice louder than before, and Calib imagined the Two-Legger peering one last time into the saddlebag. Calib felt for his rucksack, hoping he'd thought of everything.

"Keep an ear out, too, for news," Galahad continued. "We need to know how bad it's gotten in other villages."

There was a soft grunt and a thud as Bors settled into the saddle.

"Stay safe," Galahad said.

"You, too, Galahad," Bors said. "I'm beginning to think there is more to fear within the castle than outside it."

Calib thought about Madame von Mandrake, Edwin, Warren, and all the sick they were leaving behind those walls. There was some truth to the boy's words, though to think that they were somehow running away from the illness made Calib feel guilty. He could tell by Cecily's quiet sniffling that she was thinking about her mother too.

There was a cluck, and the horse began to sway forward just as Calib remembered what he'd forgotten. He had never told Galahad that he had seen that new Two-Legger boy in the library. He unlatched the clasp on the box and peeked out from the flap in the saddlebag.

It was no use now—they had already crossed the drawbridge.

Calib sighed and breathed in the fresh dew-filled air. The moon and stars were hidden behind thick blankets of clouds. With the fear of plague, everyone was hiding in their homes to protect themselves. Even the local tavern, known for hosting revelers late into the night, had been boarded up.

All the more reason for them to seek Avalon before it was too late.

"How long until we reach the Emerald Sea?" he whispered to Cecily as she came out of the box.

"It's a two days' hard ride with the Two-Legger," Cecily responded. "But that's the easy part. Once we get there, we'll need to find a ship willing to believe that we know where Avalon is—and risk a run-in with a sea monster. Unless, of course, you want to swim there."

"Swim?" he squeaked. His mind flashed back to floundering in the moat, trying to get to Commander Kensington.

Cecily waved her paw dismissively. "All mice know how to swim."

"Maybe where you're from," he mumbled.

Bors urged his horse into a gallop as they reached open fields. Cecily and Calib secured themselves in the satchel by wrapping their tails around the buckles of the bag. The sea flew by them on the right, the air heavy with the scent of salt. A sliver of dawn appeared on the horizon, casting everything around them in a pink, hazy glow. After an hour of steady travel, the road began to curve into the woods.

Bors slowed his horse to a trot. Most in Camelot

revered the Darkling Woods as an unfathomable realm, full of secrets and strange wonders. The ancient trees had grown unruly and tall, threatening to overcome the path at times. From above, the branches hovered like threatening limbs. It was enough to put even a Two-Legger ill at ease. Bors began to shakily whistle a merry tune.

A sudden yell brought Calib and Cecily to full attention. They poked their heads out of the bag.

Three dark shapes leaped from the bushes. Two-Leggers! And—judging from their all-black clothing, fabric masks, and wicked-looking knives—highwaymen.

"Seems we've netted us a young noble today, lads!" one of the masked men said. "That'll bring in a mighty ransom!"

Calib gave Cecily a panicked glance. His grip on his father's sword was unsteady from sweat. He'd never had to attack a Two-Legger before, unless he counted that time he'd scared cranky old Sir Edmund.

"Wait," Cecily mouthed back, her paw on her sword's hilt. "Back in the box."

"In the name of Camelot, I command you to stand down!" Bors shouted. "I am on official business for King Arthur!"

The highwayman laughed. "We answer to no king but the one stamped on your coins."

"That is treasonous talk." It would have sounded

impressive, Calib thought, if Bors's voice hadn't wavered.

"My loyalty lies with my hungry children first," one of the men said gruffly. "Now hand over the gold."

Two of the highwaymen rushed Bors from each side. With an ear-piercing neigh, the horse reared. Calib heard the leather strap holding the medicine box to the saddle snap.

"Brace yourself!" he shouted as the entire world upended. Bottles clinked as the box spun in the air and landed with a bone-bruising thud into the mud.

"Are you all right?" Cecily cried over the thunderous hoofbeats that slammed into the ground and then quickly faded away.

"Fine!" Calib shouted back. "The straw helped with the landing. But it sounds like our ride to Poole is gone." He pressed his ear to the box.

"What do I have to tell you?" one of the highwaymen snarled outside. "Always grab the reins first! We just lost a perfectly good horse!"

"Not to mention the ransom we would have gotten for the boy," the second thief said. "A Camelot ransom would have fed us for weeks."

"Well, at least he dropped something," responded another.

Calib and Cecily dove into the straw, and not a moment too soon. The lid above them lifted. The highwayman's fingers sifted through the box. Calib waited for just the right moment. . . .

"Yow!" The man yelped as Calib rushed out and brought his sword down on the man's knuckles. "This box is infested with vermin!"

Pain exploded in front of Calib's eyes as the man grabbed him by his tail. His entire body was yanked upward, and the ground spun away dizzyingly. He squirmed and struggled, trying to reach his captor's hand with his sword. Where was Cecily?

The Two-Legger peered at Calib for a second before throwing the mouse inside an earthenware jar that had recently held some sort of strong drink. It reeked of a sickly sweet juice.

"Ow! There's another one!"

A moment later, something soft and heavy landed on Calib. He could just make out the white fur trimming Cecily's ears before a lid closed over them, submerging them in a sticky darkness.

"Ow! Sorry, sorry," Cecily said as she scooted off him. "Did I hurt you?"

"No, but the fall nearly dislocated my tail." Calib gingerly felt around for broken bones but thankfully found none. "I think I'm all right. You?"

"Fine."

Calib heard her claws click against the hard clay. And

though he couldn't see her, he sensed her feeling the walls of their prison, looking for a weak spot. They no longer heard the Two-Leggers' voices. They must have given up and gone looking for new prey.

"I found a crack!" Cecily exclaimed a minute later. "Help me make it bigger."

Calib hurried to her side and together, they banged the pommels of their swords against the inside of the jug.

Cha-clunk!

Calib lurched back from the wall as an echoing thud filled the jug. He threw up his paws and plugged his ears. What was happening?

Another thud, and the jug shattered.

Calib quickly rolled into a ball and covered his head as the earthenware pieces fell around him in big chunks. When the clattering stopped, he peeked one eye open. A familiar face grinned back at him.

"Now," Barnaby Badle said, twirling his slingshot confidently. "What was that about being helpful?"

CHAPTER 22

The pink sunrise did not sit well with Galahad. It cast a sickly sheen across everything in the garden. He hoped he had done the right thing by staying back at Camelot and sending the mice with Bors.

Part of him felt like he was missing out on a great adventure—a chance to explore the land. But when he saw Father Walter squinting to read even the simplest scrolls, Galahad knew he had made the right choice.

It was not so long ago that he wished he were anywhere else, but now the castle had become his home.

Galahad was picking his way through the marshy parts of Camelot's riverbed, hunting for mudberries. It provided some relief for those suffering from the white fever—what the nuns at St. Anne's had begun calling the illness, as it drained the color out of the sick's faces. By giving it a name, Galahad couldn't help but feel like the sickness had become an all-powerful monster.

He was mucking about on his hands and knees when he stumbled upon Queen Guinevere napping in a hammock normally reserved for the kitchen staff. Her long dark hair was tousled over her face, and her dress was wrinkled.

"Are you all right, Your Highness?" he asked.

Queen Guinevere woke up with a start. "Ah, Galahad," she said, eyeing his satchel full of berries. "Not thinking of running away again, are you?"

"No," Galahad replied truthfully. "Just helping resupply our apothecary as best we can. But what are you doing out here?"

The queen stretched and shrugged, but her eyebrows still knitted in worry. "Arthur's dreams are loud and strange, as of late. I find it hard to sleep when he's mumbling at all hours. I think the stress is wearing on him. Besides, I've been scrying with the mirror, trying to find out how the white fever could be cured."

"Any luck?" Galahad asked. He had noticed that some

of Merlin's Scrolls were missing from the full set in the library. And Galahad didn't want to admit that he was hopelessly confused by the scrolls himself.

Guinevere shook her head and rubbed her temples. The braids in her hair were messy and stuck out in different directions. Her crown, which she was rarely seen without, was still caught in the hammock netting.

"There were once things on this Earth that had great powers, but I suspect you may be wielding the last great miracle of our time." Guinevere sighed wistfully, eyeing Excalibur. "The rest of us will have to make do with berries and herbs."

Galahad placed a protective hand over the hilt of the sword. Sometimes, more than anything, he wanted to share Excalibur's secrets with someone who might understand it. But these days, with so many prying ears about, it was still too dangerous.

"There's something I've been wanting to ask," he began, hesitant. "It's the king's nephew. He seems . . . fine, I guess, but he makes me uncomfortable with some of his questions . . . ," he began.

"Be careful with that one," Guinevere said, unhooking her crown from the hammock. "Red is trickier than you might expect. But with a mother like his, the boy's had a harder path than most."

"Morgan le Fay?" Galahad asked, remembering what

Red said about his mother talking to snakes.

"Arthur's half sister." Guinevere stood and straightened her gown. "She abandoned Red to seek Avalon's priestesses. Red grew up moving around from relation to relation. Arthur had lost all track of him until just a few months ago."

Galahad nodded. While he took heart that someone else in Camelot didn't think Red was Merlin's gift to the castle, he also felt a pang of guilt. He too knew what it was like to feel abandoned by a parent.

"Ah, just the two people I was looking for!"

Galahad turned to see Sir Lancelot striding determinedly through the thicket. Even when his father was dressed in his regular day robes, he looked regal and capable. His jaw was set and his gray eyes were alert, and only a small sheen of sweat indicated that Sir Lancelot had put forth any effort on this warm spring day. Galahad tried to mimic his father's posture, certain and strong.

"Your Highness," Lancelot said, bowing to the queen. "Arthur requests your presence at the Round Table."

The queen gave him a searching look. "Is he all right?"

"The king is fine," Sir Lancelot assured. "The remaining knights and their staff are threatening to leave the castle for fear of the sickness."

Queen Guinevere sighed and tried to pin her braids and crown back in place. "Of course they are. None of them ever stop to think about anyone except for themselves—that they will only spread the sickness if they leave. I'll address them now."

As the queen swept out of the garden, Lancelot turned his attention to his son. Galahad winced as he saw his father take in his dirty clothes and muddy hands.

"And you, young sir, look like you've been mucking in the stables."

Galahad, thinking his father would be upset if he knew that he'd spent most of the afternoon rooting through the mud instead of doing something more befitting a du Lac, furtively pushed his bag behind him.

"I've been sparring with Red in the training grounds," he lied.

"Very good," said Lancelot. "That Red is a good sparring partner for you. When the Saxons eventually return, you'll be ready."

But as soon as Queen Guinevere was out of sight, Lancelot's shoulders suddenly hunched over, and he began to sway. It was then that Galahad saw his father's face was dangerously pale.

"Would you ask Father Walter to come see me? I'm afraid I'm not well."

"Father!" Galahad said, catching Sir Lancelot before he fell to the ground.

CHAPTER 23

Relief and a tingle of embarrassment rolled off Calib's back as he brushed the last of the clay dust from his fur.

"Have you been following us this entire time?" he demanded of Barnaby, who remained standing, grinning widely.

Barnaby shrugged and offered Calib a paw to help him up. "I'm tired of being left behind, so I asked Valentina to help me tail you!"

A dark shadow swooped over them as the Darkling

crow perched on a nearby tree. Calib could barely see her. As the head scout for the Stormwings, a Darkling clan, Valentina wore a new cape of sable wool that allowed her to blend in with the trees.

"Good thing we arrived when we did," Valentina said. "The thieves ran when I dove for their eyes."

"Some sneaky planners we are," Cecily mumbled, her ears slightly pink, and Calib knew she was embarrassed that they'd let two creatures trail them so easily.

"What happened to the Two-Legger?" Calib asked. "He was supposed to be our ride."

"He's long gone," Valentina said. "He galloped ahead, like a wildfire was chasing him."

Calib cursed their bad luck. "It will take us weeks to get to Poole by paw," he said.

"Maybe more . . . ," Cecily said in dismay.

"Is that where those ley lines told you to go?" Barnaby asked.

After sharing what he and Cecily learned, Barnaby looked thoughtful. "Maybe Valentina could fly us," he suggested.

"I'm not strong enough to carry all three of you," Valentina said, ruffling her feathers.

"It would be an awfully large bird who could carry three mice," Cecily said, nibbling her claws.

"Unless . . . ," Valentina said. Suddenly, she threw out

her wings and cawed. "Unless it's not a bird at all! I know who can help— Ruby owes you a favor."

"Who?" Calib asked, surprised. He'd never even heard of the name.

But Valentina's wing had already pushed down and launched her into the air. The rest of the group quickly gathered their belongings and jogged to keep up with the crow's shadow.

"Who's Ruby?" Cecily called out.

The crow did a slow circle above them. "If I told you, you might not like it."

The mice tailed Valentina from the morning through most of the afternoon, running until they thought their paws might give out from beneath them. Calib was just about to call out for a break when the crow shouted from the branches above them.

"I can see her den from here—just a little more!"

Barnaby glanced at Cecily and Calib with worry. "What kind of creatures live in dens?"

"There are no bears left," Calib said quietly, thinking of Berwin. "Maybe badgers? Or—"

"Foxes!" Cecily interrupted breathlessly, and pointed. Calib could just make out the flash of red fur through a scraggly bush. No *wonder* Valentina hadn't told them.

He wanted to yell at the crow, but he also didn't want

to attract the foxes' attention. All the Darklings had their tails to the mice and hadn't noticed them . . . yet.

"What do we do now?" Barnaby whispered, biting his pawnails.

Calib listened for Valentina's response, but none came. She'd disappeared.

"Wait, I think," Calib guessed. "Cecily, you should—Where are you going?"

The mouse-maid had sneaked forward a few more paces.

"I want to know what's got them all distracted," she said without stopping. "It's poor formation to let others sneak up on you. It could cost you in battle."

Calib and Barnaby looked at each other in exasperation—being caught by surprise earlier had really rankled her tail—but they crept after her.

The foxes had all gathered under the branches of a very large, blackened oak tree. It looked like lightning had struck it recently; the ground around still a scorched brown. And in front of the trunk was a group of performers. They were the strangest creatures Calib had ever seen, and bundled in raggedy jackets and cloaks. It was near impossible to tell what sort of animals they were.

"Are you ready to witness a miracle?" the tallest one roared in a gravelly voice. A macabre headdress made out of a bird's skull decorated her head. "I am the great Mistress Pearl, and we are the Troubadours, the scrappiest traveling magicians and healers this side of the Iron Mountains." She bowed deeply, and the other four followed suit.

Scrappy is one way to put it, Calib thought. Mistress Pearl's eyes were thickly charcoaled, creating the appearance of a mask. She wore an outfit that looked like layers and layers of tattered silk wrapped around her body, making her seem bigger than she actually was. The others weren't much better off. Their clothes might have once belonged to animals two times too small.

Cecily concealed herself behind a small rock, just off to the side of the trunk. Calib and Barnaby quickly slunk toward her.

"Prepare to be astounded!" said another member of the company. This one wore a jester's cap that hung low over his eyes. Every time he moved, the bells jangled. "As we are about to bring this dead tree . . . back . . . to . . . LIFE!"

Mistress Pearl pulled a wooden wand from inside her robe pocket. It was about the size of a Two-Legger toothpick.

Calib watched skeptically as Mistress Pearl waved her paws over the tree's trunk. She mumbled some unintelligible words, and the other four repeated them. As Mistress Pearl's movements grew more and more wild, their chanting grew louder. Soon, even the foxes were looking at one another in confusion.

Calib frowned. Was the fortune-teller making fun of them?

Suddenly, a new branch began sprouting from a crevice where the trunk had split. Perfectly unburned and growing faster than seemed possible, the branch unfurled rows of new green leaves. The gentle scent of rosemary lingered in the air, lulling everyone into a gentle trance.

"That's incredible!" Calib gasped. Not one of Sir Alric's many inventions could do anything like that. With some effort, Mistress Pearl detached one of the leaves from the dead branch and handed it to a nearby fox.

"This wand can do many miraculous things," Mistress Pearl said, her voice dipped low and mysterious. "It can draw out life where there was death, health out of sickness!"

Calib's whiskers twitched as he tried to contain his sudden excitement. After a terrible day on the road, had the solution to their quest just landed in front of them?

Mistress Pearl and her fellow travelers were rushed by the foxes, who all seemed to have been struck by the same idea.

"Visit my youngest kit! She's had a wet nose for days. . . ."

"Does your wand protect against the plague?" another asked.

Plague? Calib's stomach turned. This was the first time

Calib had heard the sickness described as such. It slid into his mind like a knifepoint, lodging with cold certainty. Time was against them.

"Yes, yes," Mistress Pearl said, waving her paws for calm. She hopped onto the dead branch. "Each of you may hold the wand and make one healing wish."

Calib's paws darted out from behind the rock, and before he knew what he was doing, he heard his own voice rise above the crowd.

"Come to Camelot!" he shouted. "We have many sick!"

Mistress Pearl's charcoaled eyes fell on Calib, but hers weren't the only pair.

A spring breeze ruffled his fur, and he was suddenly very aware of how quiet the grove had become. Slowly, he looked up to find all the foxes were staring at him, their fangs bared.

CHAPTER 24

Calib's bravery shriveled away. He glanced behind him to see Cecily and Barnaby still watching him from the rock. His heartbeat slowed when he saw Cecily quietly unsheathe her sword and Barnaby fit a pebble in his sling—but only a fraction. What could mice-sized swords do against foxes with fur still thick from winter?

"A Camelot mouse!" spat a gray fox with narrow eyes. "And who gives you the *right* to stride in and take a healer visiting *us*? What makes a castle dweller better than those who forage in the woods?"

Calib gulped slightly, his eyes sliding to his friends again before he could stop himself. And this time, the foxes noticed. A vixen of brackish brown was next to Cecily and Barnaby before he could even blink.

"Come on, share the bounty," the brown one said, circling Barnaby and Cecily from behind. "We just want a taste of fine Camelot cuisine. Judging from the size of ye, there's plenty to go around."

"Hey!" Calib said. "Leave my friends alone." He was vaguely aware of the troubadours retreating into their tent, not wanting to get in the fray.

The two lean foxes snarled, emitting a high-pitched screech that hurt Calib's ears.

"This is just like Camelot," the brown one snapped. "Play nice when you need saving from the Saxons, but it's business as usual when you don't need us anymore!"

Calib's paws clenched. Why had Valentina brought them here if the foxes didn't trust the castle?

"We ought to teach you a lesson on sharing." The second fox bared her teeth and let out another earsplitting hiss.

"And I ought to teach *you* a better lesson on manners," a new, throaty voice cut through the noise.

Calib's head snapped around to see a vixen with burnished copper and black fur. She had appeared without warning behind the two foxes. Streaks of green paint covered the fox's coat, and she carried a spear slung across her back.

With one swift movement, the vixen grabbed an ear on each creature and yanked up.

"Ow, ow, ow, sorry, Chief Ruby!" one yelped as both of them were forced to stand on their hind legs.

"Didn't realize they were under your protection," said the other, standing on his tiptoes, trying to keep his balance.

"They are, as decreed by Leftie the Lynx after the Battle of the Bear," Ruby said, baring her teeth. "Now be gone with you!"

The bullies slunk away, turning tail and retreating into the woods. Slowly, the crowd began to disperse.

"My apologies for the behavior of my clan," the fox said. "I am Ruby, chieftain of the Southwood foxes. Many of us are not used to treating Camelot as allies quite yet. Six months of peace is not so long compared to decades of war."

Barnaby bowed, followed by Calib. Cecily still simmered, but she managed a half curtsy. There was a flutter out of the corner of Calib's eye, and he saw Valentina land on the lightning-struck tree.

"As you can see, these mice are an honorable sort," the crow said. "They've saved my life—and yours by association, so you owe them much."

Ruby studied them with piercing golden eyes. For a moment, Calib wondered what kind of recipes might call for mouse bones and tails.

"I will escort them to Poole, but only to the outskirts," the fox chieftain finally said, lowering her head in a slight bow. "Two-Legger towns aren't friendly to foxes. We will leave at first light."

The vixen turned to leave, but Cecily called out, "Chief Ruby, if I may . . . Who were those troubadours working their magic?"

Ruby scowled over in the direction of Mistress Pearl, who'd just appeared from a rather cozy-looking tree hollow, where Calib could make out a litter of fox kits. Ruby spat on the ground.

"Charlatans, that's what they are," she said. "Newly arrived before you. My clansfolk needed the entertainment."

"But they're more than entertainers," Barnaby protested. "They're healers. I saw it with my own eyes!"

"Eyes can be fooled," Cecily said grimly. "Haven't we learned that in sword training?"

"We also learned to look at all the options," Calib said, hurt by the scorn in her voice. He had thought it was a good idea to invite Mistress Pearl to Camelot. He *still* thought it was.

"Just because she managed to make a green leaf appear from a tree, doesn't make her a qualified healer," Cecily insisted. "I've seen Maman at work. The body doesn't mend that easily."

Ruby growled low in her throat. "I would have had my warriors chase them off days ago, but these illusions seem to give my people hope, and that is a rare thing."

Hope. Calib's heart trembled. He, too, would like to bring some of that to Camelot.

That night, when the rest of the animals were asleep in their tents, Calib tossed and turned, dissatisfied with having missed his opportunity to send Mistress Pearl to the castle. His father, Sir Trenton, wouldn't have let a small thing like a friend's judgment stop him from doing something good for his home.

The mouse sat up in his sleeping sock. Grabbing some paper and ink from Barnaby's pack, Calib scribbled a letter to Commander Kensington by moonlight. Checking one last time to make sure his friends were still sleeping soundly, he stepped outside.

Most of the foxes had gone underground into their dens to sleep, so it was easy to see where Mistress Pearl and her troubadours camped. But when he arrived, their fire was only coals, and the sitting stones around it were empty.

"I had hoped you would come," said a soft voice in the dark.

Calib jumped and stifled a shout. His pulse steadied only once he saw who it was.

"M-Mistress P-Pearl," he stammered. "You're in the business of healing people, yes?"

"Of course," she said. "It is only my true calling."

"Well, there just so happens to be many sick in Camelot. We're trying to find a cure for the sickness, but we could use your help."

"We certainly could spare a stop in our travels, but I don't know that we'd be allowed in during this quarantine we've heard talk of."

"You will with this letter." Calib held up a rolled piece of parchment. Mistress Pearl took it, the red embers reflecting in her pupils. She smelled lightly of lavender.

"I can't accompany you to Camelot, but if you show it to a mouse named Devrin at the moat, it should give you and your group safe passage into Camelot Castle," Calib said in a rush. "Will you help them?"

"We live to serve and heal," Mistress Pearl replied, placing a bandaged paw over her heart. "It would be an honor for us to help your people."

Calib felt a weight lift from his shoulders. "Thank you," he whispered.

"You're doing the right thing, Calib," Mistress Pearl

said, patting his shoulder. "Now to bed before we wake the others."

He nodded and left the troubadours' dying flames. When he returned to his tent, he saw that Cecily and Barnaby still slept soundly. As he drifted into sleep, something struck him as funny . . . but his sleepy mind couldn't quite hold on to its thoughts.

It came to him at the last moment before he slipped into sleep: he had never told Mistress Pearl his name.

CHAPTER 25

When they woke, Mistress Pearl and her troubadours were already gone. Secretly, Calib felt pleased by what he had done. After a hasty breakfast, the three mice climbed aboard Ruby and began their journey farther south.

Calib thought he would never again experience the thrill of riding on Howell, but despite being half the size of a wolf, the fox moved just as fast. As Ruby leaped through the underbrush of the woods at a light-footed pace, it was all the mice could do to cling on to the thin leather harness she had fashioned for them.

They traveled for three weary days, stopping only for a few hours of sleep in the evening and quick bites to eat. Most of the ride was spent in silence, as all the mice needed to reserve their strength for holding on to Ruby. Calib's muscles were so sore, he thought his arms might fall off his shoulders.

On the third day, Ruby braked near a stream. Cecily and Barnaby quickly ate their sunflower seeds, then ran into the stream for a refreshing dip. But Calib, still wary around water, slowly nibbled on a seed, careful not to move too much. Ruby sunbathed next to him, clearly enjoying the momentary rest.

A songbird trilled nearby, and Calib was reminded of their good-byes to Valentina, who had flown back to Camelot days before.

"Remember your promise, Ruby Torntail," she had warned the fox before she took off into the tree branches. "You owe this mouse a great deal."

"Contrary to popular belief, we foxes know when to be straightforward," Ruby had replied. "Your mouse friends are safe with me."

Now Calib swallowed his sunflower seed. "Ruby, what did Valentina mean when she said you owed me?" he asked. "I've never met you before in my life."

Ruby looked down at Calib in surprise. "You? I don't

believe I owe you anything. My debt is to Cecily von Mandrake."

"What?" Calib asked, the question leaving his mouth before he could stop it.

The fox flashed a sharp-toothed smile. "At the Battle of the Bear, when I was pinned down by two weasels, that little mouse managed to draw one away. Saved my life, actually, and for that, I consider it an honor to aid in her next quest."

Calib's insides curdled from embarrassment. He'd spent so much of his time assuming they were on *his* quest to find the cure, he'd forgotten that Cecily was the one who'd set them on it. Was Cecily right, then? Was he taking credit for heroic acts that weren't his to take?

"Are we ready?" Cecily called out, and Calib jumped. He hadn't realized she'd returned from washing her paws in the stream. As they resumed their spots on Ruby's back, he wondered if she'd heard their conversation, but the rushing wind was too loud to ask.

They smelled the port town of Poole even before it came into view.

A smoky, fishy scent wafted up from the hill they had climbed. An expanse of rust-colored roofs curving like a crescent moon along a cerulean bay greeted them. Scores of ships in every size, from schooners to cargo ships, were docked at port.

A heaviness settled around Calib's shoulders. Surely one of those many ships would be willing to take them on . . . right?

"This is where I leave you," Ruby said, and the mice slid down her tail. The fox bowed, flourishing her long tail. "Good luck, young mice. Do not hesitate to call on the Southwood clan should the need arise."

"Thank you, Miss Ruby," Barnaby said. "Hopefully, we won't have to." They waved good-bye, and the fox became a red streak retreating back into the forest.

The three traveled the rest of the way by paw. By the time the sun officially set beyond the horizon, the trio was already exhausted from their day of hard and steady travel.

They walked up to the city gates, the only opening in a sturdy wall that seemed to run for miles on both sides, curving along the bay. There were two entrances, one for Two-Leggers, and a smaller one for creatures, tucked to the side where there was a missing stone.

A mean-looking hare with tattoos in the shape of ocean waves guarded the gate. He eyed them up and down with a suspicion. "Now where you lot from? And what business d'ye have in Poole?"

Calib hoped his tunic with the Christopher crest was hidden well underneath his cloak. He opened his mouth to speak when Barnaby interrupted him.

"We're jis here to meet me mum at the inn. Been tradin' with the Darklin's for supplies, y'see?"

Cecily and Calib blinked. They'd never heard Barnaby speak like that, though his accent matched the hare's perfectly.

The hare relaxed but wasn't entirely convinced. "Well, youse shouldn'a be dressed like that if you know what's good for you."

"What d'ye mean?" Barnaby asked.

"You look like you're a bunch of northern folk with those cloaks o' yours. And that's where the plague is. Imma supposed to turn those types away."

"Nay, we've jis been over the woods yonder, no furtha," Barnaby reassured him. "These clothes were from a trade Papa made with some Camelot folks three seasons ago."

"Is that so?" The hare narrowed his eyes at Calib and Cecily. He prayed the hare wouldn't ask *them* a question.

Finally, after what felt like ages, the hare stepped aside and let them through onto the busy streets of Poole.

"Take care, mouslin's; these are dangerous times."

The three were smiling giddily as they passed through the gate.

"How did you learn to do that, Barnaby?" Cecily asked, impressed.

Barnaby shrugged. "I scavenge food from the marketplace and hear a lot of accents. I kind of have an ear for these things. My French isn't so bad either: *Ma nourriture préférée est le fromage.*"

"*Bon travail!*" Cecily said. "Cheese is my favorite food too."

"Well, you just saved our tails, that's for sure," Calib said, grinning from ear to ear. He thumped Barnaby on the back, who beamed in return.

It was strange to see a city other than Camelot, which Calib had come to know like the back of his paw. Snippets of foreign languages drifted into Calib's ears. The Two-Leggers spoke strangely here, with clipped words.

"Can you believe it? I was born here," Cecily whispered, wonder in her voice.

Such lively bustle and excitement had long abandoned Camelot with the onset of the sickness. These days, Calib's home felt more like a tomb. The thought hollowed out his chest.

They followed the main street to the marina, where Barnaby suddenly stopped and sniffed the air. "Do you smell that? Smells like dinner."

Calib took a deep breath: under the heavy smell of sea and fish lingered another scent, one of cinnamon-laced bread and tangy, savory meat. Their stomachs collectively growled.

"It smells . . . familiar." Cecily's nose twitched. "I think I *know* those spices. This way!"

She weaved between wooden crates, dodging careless Two-Legger boots with ease.

"Where are we going?" Calib asked, trying to keep pace.

"I'm not sure," she admitted. "I'm just following my nose."

"My paws hurt," Barnaby complained. "Do you think we could rest at that tavern over there?"

Calib looked to see Barnaby pointing to a nearby house with pink shutters and a friendly sign with bold white lettering that read "Thom's Tavern." Scanning over the tavern's stucco facade, Calib spied a little mouse-sized door right next to the larger one for Two-Leggers. A smaller sign on that door read "Tiny Thom's Tasty Tavern."

Cecily's eyes widened. "There . . ."

"Then let's go!" Barnaby said, walking faster than he had all day. "I'm *hungry*."

Calib and his friends swung open the tavern door, and a gust of greasy cooking smells puffed out. They entered a cozy room lined with wooden tables and stools with cracked cups, but it was the walls that caught Calib's attention.

The walls were *covered* with maps. Maps of islands, castles, mountains—even a map of a fantasyland called Vinland that was rumored to be beyond the Sapphire Sea. Some were tattered while others had crisp corners, but all of them had *x*'s on them.

Treasure maps. This was a place for Poole's famous treasure hunters!

A gray-furred badger wearing a red woolen vest walked toward them from the bar. He had to duck to avoid the lowest ceiling beams.

"Welcome to the Tasty Tavern!" the badger said. He carried two tankards of mead in each paw, and some of the amber liquid splashed out as he came to a stop in front of them. "What can I do for you fine travelers this eve—"

The old badger's jaw went slack, as if he had seen a ghost. His paws shook, and drink dribbled out onto the sawdust floor. "Good heavens," he cried. "Viviana, is that you?"

CHAPTER 26

Cecily's eyes went equally wide. "Master . . . ," she paused, and Calib could see her searching for a long-buried memory. Her eyes suddenly lit up. "Master Basil! I'm Viviana's daughter, Cecily!"

Calib jumped as the badger slammed his tankards down and howled in laughter. Everyone in the tavern turned to face him. "Liliana, come in here!" he called. "You're not going to believe this!"

A wizened old vole with a tattered chef's hat poked her head out from the kitchen.

"What is it, Basil, I'm busy— Oh my whiskers!" The vole's eyes widened as big as peas, and her paws came up to her face in surprise. Both of them launched into a tirade of questions and exclamations, pulling Cecily in closer to have a better look.

"Why it's been a near lifetime! You were this tall last time I saw ye!"

"How is Viviana? Why"—the old vole blinked rapidly behind her glasses at Cecily, who had suddenly burst into tears—"whatever is the matter?"

"Thank you," Cecily said, accepting the dishrag Basil thrust under her nose. She dabbed at her sudden tears. "It's just, Maman is very sick, along with many others."

"Where is she?" the vole exclaimed. "We'll go right to her."

"She's at Camelot," Cecily mouthed as quiet as she could. Basil and Liliana gasped softly. A few of the rats near the door also turned to stare.

"Sit," the badger said, taking a sniffling Cecily under his arm. He quickly swiped hot mugs of cider from a tray and handed them out among the three mice. "We didn't know you lot were all from Camelot. We've heard . . . well, just terrible rumors."

"What have you heard?" Calib asked. His thoughts flitted to Mistress Pearl. By his guess, they should be nearing the castle soon.

"We heard a plague called the white fever has turned the place into a ghost town and that the whole castle is vulnerable," Basil whispered, his deep voice coming out in gentle grumbles. "The usual elixirs don't work, and no one has seen the likes of it before."

The three mice's expressions went slack at once. They looked at one another in confusion.

"But it's only been a week!" Barnaby cried. "Illnesses can't move that fast!"

"Rumors only, of course," Liliana interjected quickly. "Basil, how many times have I told you not to listen to any of that nonsense? Here, let me get you all a pastry. . . ."

Calib sat back in his chair and tried not to let Basil's words sink in too deep. Should they turn back? It didn't seem right that Camelot should suffer while they were here, sipping warm drinks in a cozy adventurers' den.

"We need to get onto a ship tonight," Cecily said grimly. "We have no time to waste."

"We're on a quest," Barnaby said to Basil, loudly enough that surrounding tables could hear, "to find a cure for Camelot."

Calib jabbed Barnaby in the side. Admitting to coming from a plague-ridden castle was a recipe for disaster. Besides, announcing your quest to everyone was no way of going about an actual quest.

"Actually," he said, casting a glare at Barnaby, "we are

trying to get to Avalon—just to ask a few questions."

"Avalon," Basil said almost reverently. "I haven't heard that word in a long time. Most treasure hunters have given up finding that mysterious island. What do you know of Avalon, mouslings?"

"Why are you speaking of Avalon, Basil?" Liliana had come back with steaming pastries. "No good has ever come from searching for that place."

"Why not?" Barnaby asked, eyes wide above his fish pie.

"Because the island doesn't want to be found."

Tugging a whisker, Calib asked, "What do you mean?"

"Strong magic hides the island from plain sight," Liliana said, voice low. "More treasure hunters than I can count on my paws have attempted this quest, but they've all run afoul of the sea. Get too close, and a storm will knock you off course or a strange beast will pull you to your watery grave."

Calib gulped. "But if no one's ever seen it, how do we know the island exists?" he asked, voice a little too shrill for a hero. Or anyone, for that matter. "Surely *someone* has come back."

Liliana shot a questioning glance toward Basil, but the badger immediately shook his head.

"But it's for Viviana," Liliana admonished.

"It's too dangerous!" the badger growled.

Cecily spread her paws wide. "Please," she said, "please tell us. Think of my mother, Viviana!"

The pity on Basil's face made Calib want to look away. Finally, the badger heaved a sigh. "You'll want to have words with Captain Tristan over yonder. He's the only creature alive who claims to have set paw on Avalon." He pointed to what looked to be a breathing stack of rags, stuffed in a corner booth.

Cecily stared at the pile in horrified fascination. "*That's* alive?"

As if on cue, the rags shifted and moved. A long black snout and a pair of pink ears emerged as Captain Tristan took a sip of his drink. He was in dire need of a bath, his fur patchy and gray with salt.

"Don't be put off by his looks," Liliana chided. "He's the best hunter Poole has ever had—or at least, he was."

"What do you mean, 'was'?" Calib asked.

Liliana shrugged. "One could say he's obsessed with Avalon. He's stopped looking for treasure in order to concentrate on finding that legendary isle again. He's lost many a crew member to his dreams and delusions of grandeur. The quest for glory can do strange things to creatures."

Calib thought Liliana looked at him a little too long as she said that last part, and he shifted uncomfortably in his seat.

"Then we should ask while he's awake," he said, and gulped down his mushroom pasty in two bites. He and Cecily stood, and, leaving behind Barnaby with two fish pastries and happy tears in his eyes, approached the treasure hunter.

"Excuse me." Calib tapped the rat's shoulder gingerly. "Do you have a moment?"

The rat instinctively drew his weapon, a strange-looking dagger that widened at the center. "Whatever you think I did, or whoever you think I wronged, it wasn't me," Captain Tristan growled. He bared his teeth, showing off two that were wrapped in gold.

"Treat our guests with respect, Captain," Basil warned from behind the bar. "One of them has her roots here."

"We're just three adventurers," Calib said, gesturing to include Barnaby at the table. "We need to head south on a ship. We're keen workers and, um . . . lean eaters."

Captain Tristan scratched his long snout and burped loudly. "Landlubbers like you would not last a day on the *Salty Pup.*"

He stood up from his bench, and Calib stepped back from the stench that rolled off him in a wave. The rat was nearly twice as tall as Calib, and twice as wide. His long tail bore a spiraling snake tattoo. "Now if you'll excuse me, I'm in need of a bath before I set sail."

"But you're seeking Avalon, aren't you?" Cecily asked. She stepped forward and offered him a newly refilled cup of mead. "We know how to get to Avalon, but we just need a ship and a seaworthy guide."

"*Of course* you know the way to Avalon, mouse babe," Tristan said, sarcasm dripping thick as honey. "Your nursemaid told pretty stories—now run along."

"But we do," Calib insisted. "We figured out the ley lines!"

Captain Tristan stilled. When he spoke next, an unexpected ferocity laced his words. "What else do you know?" He bared his incisors.

Calib drew back even farther. They *didn't* know anything else, but he wasn't about to let this smelly sea rat know that.

"Well?" Tristan growled. "Speak up! That island is mine to find!"

"We know enough," Calib pushed out, trying his hardest not to stammer. The rat didn't look like a pile of rags anymore. He looked strong and cunning, and Calib was suddenly very aware of the sea captain's bulk. Calib cast his mind about, trying to think what the captain would want to know. He landed on what worried him the most. "We know how to defeat the Beast of Avalon!"

Tristan looked at him, agog. "You do not," he said.

"We do to!" Cecily chimed in, and Calib was grateful for how quickly his friend had caught on.

"Tell me," Tristan demanded.

"Not until we're onboard your ship," Calib said. "Take us with you as part of your crew, and we can work together to get to Avalon." It wasn't a lie, he told himself. They'd figure it out. There had to be *some* clue in the poem.

The rat eyed them, suspicious. "I will not share my treasure with mousebabes."

"Owl's teeth, we don't *want* your treasure," Calib said, exasperated. "We just want answers."

Tristan grew silent, his mind seemingly lost in thought. "Can you cook?" he asked, addressing Cecily.

"I can fight *and* cook," she replied, with a defiant scowl.

"And what about your hungry companion yonder?" He jerked his head toward Barnaby.

Calib lifted his chin. "We've all been trained in combat."

"And you can all swim?"

Calib's pulse quickened, but he nodded.

"We have a deal. The *Salty Dog* sails at midnight," Captain Tristan said. He stood up and stretched, the reek of many days' sweat rolling off him. "I hope you know what you're signing up to do."

He parted some of his rags aside to bare his chest.

A large pink gash ran across it like a sash. It was only recently healed.

"It's not many who choose the seafaring way of life willingly," the old captain added. "And the path to Avalon is treacherous beyond your imagining."

CHAPTER 27

Galahad paced outside the door to Sir Lancelot's chambers. Father Walter had been in there for what felt like hours. Surely he would be able to tell by now whether it was white fever that had stricken his father.

At first, Galahad had insisted that he stay with the knight, but Father Walter soon sent him outside.

"Your worrying will do you no good," he had said.

So Galahad waited, and he tried to focus on the latest of Merlin's Scrolls he had taken out of the library. All the words seemed to run together in this one, and everything was written in the same strange code. Galahad briefly wondered if Excalibur might help him understand the code in the same way it helped him understand animals.

He was just reaching for his sword when a pair of rapid footsteps echoed down the hall. Galahad looked up to see Red and King Arthur walking toward him.

"Ah, Galahad," King Arthur said, looking drawn and tired while Red looked alert. "What's happened to Lancelot?"

"He's with Father Walter," Galahad said, swallowing back a lump in his throat.

"It's the plague, isn't it?" Red asked.

"That's for the healer to decide," Galahad said, with a flash of defensiveness. These days, it was hard to see King Arthur without his new shadow. Red had put a lot of effort into getting on everyone's good side, especially the king's. And now he was undeniably his favorite.

King Arthur closed his eyes and rubbed his temples.

"This is getting beyond our control. There are no more healers from the surrounding kingdoms," he said. "For now I need Walter to attend to the queen."

"Queen Guinevere?" Galahad couldn't believe his ears. He had just seen the queen earlier that evening. Could the disease truly have spread so quickly, or was it getting worse?

"Let me speak with Walter about our options at this moment," Arthur said, stepping into the room.

Galahad and Red were left outside in the hall.

"I'm sorry to hear about your father," Red said, breaking the silence.

Galahad nodded, intent on studying the patterns on the stone floor. He was afraid his emotions would betray him if he looked up. And the last person he wanted to cry in front of was Red.

"You spend a lot of time in the infirmary and the library, don't you?" Red said, picking at his fingernails. He looked up at Galahad, observing him.

"I'm doing what I can to help find the cure," Galahad said warily, not sure where Red's new line of questioning was going to lead.

"I've been looking forward to sparring with you at training," Red said. "But you're never there. If I didn't know any better, I'd say you were avoiding having to face me in combat."

"My father could be sick or d—" Galahad stopped short, unable to finish the sentence. "There are more important things to worry about than who has the faster parry!"

Red held up his hands. "I didn't mean to offend. You and I have more in common than you think, Galahad. We shouldn't work against each other."

"I didn't think we *were* working against each other," Galahad said.

"Well," Red said quietly, "I guess that depends on how much you're keeping secret."

Galahad had enough of Red's prying. He wasn't sure what he was going to do—hit Red or run down the hall—but his decision was made for him when King Arthur and Father Walter stepped out of Lancelot's room at that moment.

Galahad's anger evaporated as he saw their grim expressions. "Is Father going to be all right?"

King Arthur motioned for Red to accompany him. The older boy gave Galahad one last look before following.

Father Walter put a reassuring had on Galahad's shoulder.

"Your father is sleeping for now. He is a strong man. I very much doubt this sickness will keep him down for long." The old man tried to sound reassuring, but Galahad could see the doubt in his eyes.

CHAPTER 28

The thudding of Two-Legger boots on the gangplank reverberated like thunder in Calib's ears. The mice watched from the shadow of a large barrel as the Two-Legger sailors rolled the heavy casks up the ramp of the *Salty Dog*. The plank sagged heavily as they resupplied the barnacle-covered ship.

The sea sloshed and churned underneath their paws. Just a single piece of wood separated them from the murky moonlit water below. As they contemplated how to sneak onto the Two-Legger boat without being seen or squashed, Calib tried to quell the feeling that they were way out of their depth.

But shortly after discovering that the barrels behind them were full of Swiss cheese wheels, the mice clambered inside. Tucking himself safely into one of the holes, Calib was able—for the most part—to tamp down his nausea as Two-Leggers rolled the barrel (and three stowaway mice) up the ramp.

By the time the barrel began its jostling descent into the belly of the ship, Calib had decided he'd never eat Swiss again. He wondered if he might be the seasick type—but it was too late to do anything about it now. Suddenly, the spinning stopped.

They had arrived onboard the *Salty Dog.*

When the footsteps of the Two-Legger sailors faded away, the mice risked poking their heads out. One by one, they crawled out of the barrel.

"I don't feel so well," Barnaby mumbled from somewhere to Calib's right. Calib could feel the ground beneath his paws bob up and down with the waves. Even nimble Cecily held out a paw to right herself.

Calib let his eyes adjust to the new surroundings. They were in the belly of a ship, where all the goods were housed. It resembled Camelot's cellars, only much more disorganized. Wooden barrels and boxes were stacked haphazardly against the walls, lashed together with rope.

Small streaks of moonlight trickled in from cracks in the deck above.

His ears perked up as he detected the scuttling of many running paws coming in their direction from above and below.

"Weapons out!" Calib cried. Cecily drew her sword with such speed it was like a blur of silver. Barnaby scrambled for his sling, slotting a pebble. Calib could hear his teeth chattering.

Dark shapes swiftly moved behind them, and scattered snickers echoed above them.

"Well, that's not quite the welcome we were expecting from the newest members of our crew," called out a familiar voice. A muscular rat stepped into the moonlight.

His jet-black fur was slicked back and clean. He wore a simple but sturdy navy coat with a built-in cape. It flared dramatically behind him, giving Calib the impression of a winged bat. On his head sat a wide-brimmed hat with a seagull's down feather stuck in it.

"C-Captain Tristan?" Calib asked, not quite believing his eyes. There was no trace of the smelly, ragtag sailor from earlier.

"Welcome, young travelers," Captain Tristan said, with a mischievous grin. "You must excuse my dreadful appearance earlier at Tiny Thom's. Months at sea without a bath can turn any gentle-rat into a rascal. Now tell me how to defeat the Beast."

"Not until we set sail," Calib said, holding out for when they would be safely on the way. "Not until we are within a day outside of Avalon."

Captain Tristan stopped smiling. "That was not the deal."

One by one, torches were lit, illuminating a crowd of about twenty surly-looking creatures. Calib scanned their faces. They were predominantly sea rats, accustomed to life near water. But he also noticed a few mice and a mean-looking ferret numbering among them.

"A mouse is only as good as his word," Tristan said. In the flickering light, his scars seemed to deepen. "If I were you, I would not cross it."

Calib did not like the odds of taking on the sea rats in a fight. Nor did he like the odds if Tristan discovered that his promise had been a bluff. He needed more *time*.

"Excuse me," a small voice quavered. Barnaby stepped out next to Calib, "but Calib hasn't broken his word."

"He has, too," Tristan sneered, and smacked the ground with his tail. Calib half expected Barnaby to scuttle back behind him or faint, but he held his ground.

"All Calib promised was that he would tell you after we boarded," Barnaby squeaked. "But he didn't specify exactly what time after we boarded."

"But that was understood," Tristan snapped. "It meant now!"

Barnaby shook his head. "You know you can't change

the terms after an agreement."

Tristan threw up his paws. "Gah! Unlike you, I am a rodent of repute," he said. "The tide is pushing us out, and we don't have time to pull out the plank. Allow me to show you where you will be bunking—and thinking long and hard about the meaning of 'promise.'"

Calib let out a sigh of relief. He might not have the answer yet to the captain's question, but for now, at least, there was time to figure it out.

They followed the sea rat through the Two-Legger storeroom. All around them, Captain Tristan's sailors broke into the barrels of goods, stuffing slivers of cheese and chewed-off pieces of sausages into their own sacks and barrels.

Something inside Calib twisted as he watched the crew loot the Two-Leggers' supplies. In the castle, the mice were always careful not to take from the unopened stores, using instead the scraps from the Two Legger kitchens that would have gone to waste if not for the mice's hard work.

"We take enough to trade with the coastal villages," Captain Tristan said, noticing Calib's snout wrinkle. "Without us merchants, those beasts would starve."

The twist of worry didn't go away, but it did loosen. Once again, Calib had failed to remember how it might be difficult for those animals who didn't live near humans.

"Where are they taking everything?" Barnaby asked, eyeing two rats who were rolling a flagon of olive oil between them. They disappeared into the far recesses of the ship.

"I'll show you," said Captain Tristan with pride in his voice.

The rat led them to a beam at the hull of the Two-Legger ship, where notched pawholds allowed them to ascend. They climbed until they reached the opening of a second landing—one that was far too short to fit a Two-Legger without crouching.

"This ship is a smuggler's paradise," Tristan said. "There are secret compartments all over it."

There was a Two-Legger shore boat lying on its side, fitting neatly in this hidden landing.

Calib's jaw dropped open, and behind him, Cecily gasped.

"Behold, the *Salty Pup*," Captain Tristan said proudly. "We use the Two-Legger ship as a resupply point, but this is the true vessel I captain."

The shore boat had been retrofitted by Captain Tristan's crew into a fully functional, rodent-sized ship, like a scrap-work cog ship. Its sails were made from a Two-Legger's poncho, and its mast from a broken oar. Captain Tristan's sailors were busy loading it full of wares.

Captain Tristan led the mice to a mildewy trunk stored

at the front. With a round hole carved into one side, the trunk was sectioned off into individual rooms. Captain Tristan showed them to one that had two bunk beds.

"I'm farther down the hall," Captain Tristan said, gesturing to a closed door at the far end. "The *Salty Pup* is just about to leave the *Salty Dog*. Once we've successfully refilled our stores, we will make our own path on the open waters."

By now the steady rocking of the boat had Calib feeling quite disoriented. He grabbed the side of the bunk to stop from keeling over.

Captain Tristan gave Calib a quizzical look. "Judging by the greenish looks about ye, I suggest finding your sea legs fast."

"Just a little too many pastries and Swiss cheese is all," Calib said, trying to sound calm and collected. Outside the ship, they could hear the shouts of Two-Leggers as they pulled up the anchor and detached from the dock. Calib swallowed back the bile building up in his throat.

There would be no turning back now.

CHAPTER 29

Calib lay awake in his bunk, his stomach as tempestuous as the sea outside. To the mouse's dismay, a rodent-sized ship did not fare any better against the lolling waves than a Two-Legger vessel.

Soon after midnight, when the Two-Legger crew was just falling asleep, the creatures of the *Salty Pup* had carefully lowered their animal-sized vessel into the Emerald Sea. Hours later, Calib was convinced that going on this trip was the worst idea he'd ever had—worse, even, than when he'd gone after the owls.

Beside him, Barnaby was sound asleep, looking as comfortable as a sea-hardened sailor. Unable to focus on anything but the ship's swaying, Calib stumbled out of his bed.

He needed fresh air. If his friends noticed he was missing, he'd just say he was taking stock of their surroundings, as a good leader should . . . and not losing the contents of his stomach over the railing. Calib wobbled into the cabin corridors.

After wandering around for a few minutes, he had gotten hopelessly lost. The hallways looked identical to one another, and most of the doors only led to more bunks filled with sleeping sailors. After some unsuccessful attempts, Calib pushed open the door to what he assumed *must* be the one leading onto the deck.

Shock quickly replaced his nausea.

The room in front of him was filled to bursting with treasure—gold coins the size of his head, gleaming Two-Legger jewelry, and a cache of finely crafted rodent-sized weapons.

He rubbed his eyes to make sure he wasn't sleepwalking. When the image didn't disappear, he stepped in. A pyramid of stacked spears glinted in the dim light that spilled in from the hallway. Carefully, he drew one out. Dread trickled down his spine.

Calib would have recognized the wicked curve of the

blade anywhere. Only one army carried that kind of spear: Saxons. His mind flashed back to the one that had felled his friend, Berwin the Bear.

He stumbled back in horror, tripping over his tail and plunging into the still-open door with a thud. His tailbone throbbed, but that paled in comparison to this discovery: Captain Tristan and his crew were in league with Camelot's most powerful enemy.

"It's not what it looks like." Captain Tristan's voice cut through the dark like an arrow.

Calib whirled around, wishing he hadn't left Darkslayer back in the bunk. "Treasure hunter, my left paw!" he spat, anger making him brave. "You're a Saxon!"

"None of the sort," Captain Tristan said, indignant. "We hunt treasure, and much of it happens to be Saxon treasure, that's all." He straightened his collar.

Calib eyed the captain's new, and very expensive, clothes. "You mean you're a bunch of thieving pirates!"

Captain Tristan's demeanor shifted, and an angry shadow fell over his face. "Let's get one thing perfectly clear: the sailors of the *Salty Pup* don't raid, mousling. We're treasure hunters. Raiding is for bloodthirsty pirates. No creature gets hurt when we come collecting."

"So where did this loot come from, then?"

"I stole it from a terrible ferret," Captain Tristan said. "In all my travels, I've never met a more terrifying creature.

He wore a mask of gold and rode a hawk."

Fear frosted Calib's heart. "The Manderlean?" he asked.

"Yes." The captain fiddled with his eye patch. "The very same who attacked Camelot with a horde of Saxons this past winter."

Calib remembered the fearsome creature—cruelly curving claws and the soulless mirth—and trembled. "How did you do it?" he asked.

"Many seasons ago, I had the misfortune of accepting a job from the Manderlean." Tristan sighed. "I didn't know at the time that the ferret's mission was to amass an army, or else I would have run that creature through with a sword."

Calib didn't think a simple sword thrust would do the job, no matter how experienced Tristan was.

"We defeated the Manderlean in battle," Calib said. "There have been no reports of Saxon attacks since."

Captain Tristan shook his head. "If you fought with the Manderlean like you claim you did, then you know that look in the creature's eyes. Hate like that doesn't go away after defeat in one battle. If that foul creature is quiet now, there must be a reason. There's always a reason."

Calib wanted to believe the captain's words, but something held him back. "Why should I believe you?"

"You don't have to," Captain Tristan said crisply. "But

if you'd like to know more, follow me."

Calib didn't want to. But he couldn't see a different option. It wasn't like he could demand to be taken back to Poole at this point.

The captain led Calib onto the deck of the ship. He ran a loving paw along the base of a cogwheel that functioned as the ship's main means of navigation. Ahead, an orange-pink dawn was rising above the ocean. Around them, sailors began to emerge for their morning duties.

From his coat pocket, Captain Tristan pulled out a folded map and opened it. Along the spider markings of the British coastline were the lines similar to what Galahad had drawn. Calib wondered how the Two-Legger was faring back at the castle. Their home felt like another world away.

"All that gold in the treasury means nothing," Captain Tristan said, tapping a paw on the open map on his table. "*This* is what is truly priceless. This is Avalon."

"Where did you get this map?" Calib asked, amazed.

"The Manderlean lent it to me in order to return to Avalon. According to legend, the island is home to a powerful treasure capable of harnessing the greatest magic in Britain."

Calib's mouth dried. A weapon of that nature in the Manderlean's paws would be catastrophic. Bracing himself, he asked, "Did you find it?"

Captain Tristan shook his head. "Before we even got close, we were chased away by the Beast of Avalon. It killed four of my crew as we tried to outsail it."

Dandelion's song echoed in Calib's memory.

Avalon's beast may look back at me.
And when it eyes your company
Only Avalon's mark will let you be.

Captain Tristan closed his eyes as if he wanted to forget something, and Calib stole a glance over the ship's side. He swallowed hard at the deep, roiling waters. Taking a few precautionary steps, he shuffled away from the edge. He should have practiced his strokes more when he'd had the chance. . . .

Tristan opened his eyes, and they looked haunted. "I never did find the thing that the Manderlean wanted, so he ordered that I be put to death. I ran, but he sent his ferret assassins after me."

Opening his eyes, the rat removed his hat, and Calib understood why he liked to wear it: ugly pink slashes ran down the length of his head.

"So why *are* you agreeing to take us back there?" Calib asked.

Captain Tristan's eyes flashed. "Because I am a treasure hunter, and there can be no greater prize if the Manderlean wanted it. Plus, as I recall, *you* said you knew how to get past the Beast . . . or was that a lie to get yourself on my ship?"

Calib winced. He had just stuck his footpaw right into his mouth. "Of *course* I know how to get there!" he bluffed. "It just . . . It requires the right mark, you know. . . . Avalon's mark . . ."

"But what is *Avalon's* mark?" Captain Tristan pressed, a hungry expression on his face.

Calib gulped. Captain Tristan might not be a Saxon . . . but he wasn't what one would call a *tame* rat, either. Before Calib could figure out what to say, there was a sharp cry from a rat on deck.

"Fire!" the sailor cried, pointing.

Captain Tristan whipped out a telescope and pointed it east.

"Pirates be near," one of the sea rats muttered.

"Pick up the pace," Captain Tristan commanded as he handed the spyglass to Calib. "Go farther west! They won't have spotted us yet."

And even though the springtime sun was warm on the ship's deck, inside, Calib felt a small chill as he held the spyglass up to his eye. He squinted, and in the distance, where the horizon narrowed into a thin green strip, he could see smoke spotting the sky.

CHAPTER 30

Galahad closed the door to Sir Lancelot's room and wiped sweat from his brow. Even though it was spring—usually a time of town fairs and sowing seeds—all the fireplaces in Camelot had been lit. Father Walter's latest attempt to combat the disease was to sweat the fever out, but so far, they had only managed to make the castle unbearably stuffy.

He picked up the handles of the wheelbarrow he'd left outside in the hall and trundled toward the door that would lead him to the queen's garden. The woodcutter had only recently fallen ill, but they were already running low on the small logs that revived the flames. They would have to take a hatchet to the queen's beloved willows.

Galahad ruminated on his last encounter with Red as he navigated the wheelbarrow past the quiet stone halls. The eerie silence reminded Galahad of the crypts under St. Anne's.

The garden was a riot of vivid red and pink flowers, a cheerful rebellion against the death that surrounded them. But Galahad noticed weeds choking the blossoms. No one had time to care for plants when there were so many patients to watch over.

"Galahad!"

He jumped as he suddenly spotted King Arthur. The king had been bent over a bed of daffodils. As he stood, Galahad could see he clutched a yellow bunch in his fist.

"Your Majesty," Galahad said, sweeping a hasty bow. "What are you doing?"

He immediately winced. Though Arthur was his father's best friend, he had never been alone with the king before. He didn't really know what to say, but it definitely wasn't his place to question a king.

"I'm sorry, s-sir," he stammered, trying to fix his mistake. "I only meant—"

"Peace," King Arthur said, walking over to him. "I'm picking flowers for the queen's sickroom." A line of worry creased his forehead. "I hope they will bring her cheer."

Galahad nodded. "I'm sure they will, Your Majesty."

The king smiled at him, warm blue eyes crinkling. "Daffodils always remind me of a time when I wasn't a king—just the second son of a lesser knight. They were blooming the day Sir Kay sent me on a fool's errand to fetch his escaped hawk from the forest. I ended up finding Merlin instead."

Arthur's calloused fingers tapped against his sword hilt. "Sometimes I wonder what would have happened if I hadn't searched the woods, if I had just stayed put and picked some daffodils instead. . . ."

The king sighed, then grinned ruefully at Galahad. "But then, I suppose you wonder similar things."

Galahad absentmindedly mirrored the king and touched Excalibur's hilt. He had never been so close to the king, and he noticed that the king's hilt was similar—no, *identical*—to Excalibur's.

A question bubbled in Galahad, then burst forth, "Does your sword also give you, um, *abilities*?"

King Arthur raised his eyebrows. "Once, a long time ago, it could show me a great many things. But for years its power waned, until it was nothing more than a symbol of might."

The king nodded toward Galahad. "It was not until I saw you with Excalibur that I realized it was because the magic had chosen a new hero to take my place."

Galahad thought about Red's suggestion that maybe he was never meant to have the sword—that it was meant for someone else. He didn't feel ready to be a leader like King Arthur. He wasn't sure he even *wanted* the responsibility.

Galahad chose his next words very carefully. "How did you know what to do when the sword chose you?"

Arthur looked thoughtfully at Galahad for a long moment.

"Truth be told, I've never known. Not fully," he admitted. "In the early years, Merlin guided my hand. It was his belief that we were all part of a larger destiny—a larger story that would outlast our time on this Earth."

The undecipherable scrolls of Merlin's libraries flashed to the front of Galahad's mind. "I wish Merlin were still here. I have so many questions," he said.

"I don't believe he truly left us," Arthur said kindly. "Not as long as his dream for a peaceful kingdom is carried on by us."

Galahad wondered whether if he told Arthur about Excalibur's powers, the king could help him understand them. But before he could open his mouth, there was a rustle behind the unkempt bushes.

"Who's there?" King Arthur drew his sword, and Galahad did the same.

Red stepped out. "Uncle, I was looking for you. Sir

Kay needs to speak with you. He has a suggestion to pause all defense work until the sickness passes."

King Arthur sighed. "Duty calls." He handed the flowers to Galahad. "Would you please give these to Guinevere? Red, lead on."

King and nephew left the garden, leaving Galahad alone with the plants and empty wheelbarrow. Quickly, Galahad began to fill the wheelbarrow with twigs and sticks. But even after it was full and all the fires had been tended, he couldn't stop wondering how much Red had heard.

CHAPTER 31

"The wind's too strong!" Barnaby shouted. "We shouldn't be up here."

It had been a week into the sea voyage, and Barnaby and Calib were on crow's nest duty. At first, it had been fun to watch sky unfurl over the waters, but after hours of blue and more blue, Calib had grown bored. He'd used the time to try to think of a way to defeat the Beast and fulfill his promise to Tristan. Again, he repeated to himself the last lines of Dandelion's song:

And when it eyes your company
Only Avalon's mark will let you be.
The one who bears it, sets you free.

There was a clue there, Calib knew it. But try as he might, he couldn't make sense of the song. It seemed he needed "Avalon's mark," but where could he find that?

"Calib!" Barnaby shouted again, shaking Calib from his theories. "We need to leave!"

The ship began to sway dangerously. Barnaby pointed at the green clouds and said something else that was carried away by the wind.

"What?" Calib shouted.

"I said, it looks like—"

Suddenly, lightning opened the sky open. The accompanying thunder shook the ship.

"Rain," Barnaby finished as a downpour began to dump on the mice.

From below, the rats shouted instructions at one another and ran to lower the sails. Calib could see Cecily helping the crew crank the cogwheel so the ship could turn against the wind.

The gale picked up, and with each gust, the ship dipped toward the ocean. Calib clutched the crow's nest tightly, as wave after wave threatened to capsize the *Salty Pup.*

"We need to get out of here!" Calib looked around

for rope to secure around themselves, but there was none within easy reach. They would have to climb down.

Barnaby stood frozen to the spot, his limbs splayed out and braced against the sides of the crow's nest. His eyes were shut tight.

"Don't think," Calib said, grabbing Barnaby's shoulders and shaking them. "Just move!"

"I want to be back at Camelot! I want to go home!" Barnaby's grip on the planking was too tight for Calib to pry off.

Finally, Calib gave the trembling mouse a hard bop on the nose. *"Move or you'll die!"*

That seemed to wake Barnaby up. "Get me out of here!"

"Follow me!" Calib waited for the ship to swing back from its latest arc before climbing to the other side of the nest. After checking his footing, the mouse began his descent, pausing every few seconds as a new wave made the ship lurch sideways. Barnaby followed behind, moving much slower.

About halfway down, Barnaby paused, his eyes trained on something in the storm. Calib followed his gaze, squinting against the whipping wind and rain. At first, he didn't see anything, and then a whitish dot appeared in the distance. It looked like a bird.

It was being buffeted every which way by the storm as

it tried to make for the *Salty Pup.* In between the rolling thunder, Calib could hear the desperate cries of a baby seagull.

"Help!" Barnaby called down to the sailors below.

"There's a bird trying to land!" Calib bellowed. He saw Captain Tristan look up from the deck and follow his pointing paw. In a second, he understood.

"Quick!" the captain's voice boomed out. "Get the fisherman's net!"

Calib looked back up at the white speck fighting against the wind like a feather in a tornado. The sea would swallow the bird if nothing was done.

"Hurry!" he yelled.

He watched as Captain Tristan and his crew unfurled a fisherman's net and began stringing it up the masthead and the boom. They were trying to give the bird a better chance at grabbing something on the ship.

The gull saw what they were doing. It beat its damp wings, trying to get closer and nab the webbing with its beak or talons. But each time the gull came close, the storm pushed the boat in a different direction.

Finally, the gull grasped the last bit of the net with its claws. It tumbled down the net from exhaustion and landed on the deck with a great big thump.

Just then, an earsplitting crack sounded, and the entire ship shuddered. The masthead was breaking!

Calib watched breathlessly as the Two-Legger oar that held up the sail came crashing into the water—whipping Captain Tristan overboard with it.

"Captain!" Calib shouted, but words would do nothing to stop the plummet. He watched in horror as the sea swallowed the rat. There was a fine line between being foolish and being a hero—but the line between Captain Tristan's life and death was even thinner.

Without thinking, Calib knotted the rope around himself and launched over the deck into the roiling waters below.

The fall was longer than he expected. There was enough time to straighten his legs like a diver before he slipped into the water with a splash.

Beneath the surface, there was calm. The waves were only shadows of themselves down here; small pulls rather than suffocating crashes. But he couldn't stay in the dark forever.

Kicking, he broke the surface, only to be met with the angry slap of waves and wind. Salt stung his eyes. Debris sloshed past his snout, narrowly missing him. He grabbed on to a piece of nearby driftwood.

He was not going to drown.

He was *not* going to drown.

Calib kicked out, searching for Captain Tristan. The waves pushed back, spinning in different directions. Finally, he saw a dark shape floating a few feet away.

Captain Tristan floated faceup on the crest of a wave. Calib flung his tail toward the captain, wrapping it around his middle. Another wave threatened to overwhelm him. He could feel the knot around his own waist loosening.

He tried to tie the rope tighter while keeping a grasp on Captain Tristan. But the sea beat against them bitterly, threatening to dash Calib against the side of the ship.

If he didn't strap Captain Tristan to the rope as soon as possible, he would lose his grip. Finally, just when he felt too exhausted to keep afloat, Calib's paws fumbled together a stronger knot.

"Pull us up!" Calib screamed into the wind. Would anyone be able to hear him? He bobbed on the angry water for agelong seconds. He could no longer feels his paws or limbs. Then—

The rope pulled taut.

Calib was lifted out of the water—like a captured fish, he thought drowsily—rising to safety as his own hope swelled. They were going to make it!

And then everything went dark.

CHAPTER 32

Galahad gripped his ledger so tight, his knuckles were turning white.

"What do you mean you *lost* the medicine box?" Galahad asked, trying to keep his voice low. He looked around to make sure Red wasn't lurking nearby.

"How about 'Thanks, Bors, for risking your life to get these supplies'? Or 'I'm glad you're safe after being set upon by highwaymen'?" Bors crossed his arms and kicked a small bundle to Galahad's feet. The bottles of dried feverfew inside clanked together.

Father Walter had reassigned them all from their normal duties to help attend to the patients. For some unknown reason, the pages—and the other children of the castle under sixteen—had not contracted the white fever. Yet.

Galahad's former sanctuary in the apothecary had turned into a circus. Bottles were strewn everywhere, and dirty linens were piled in the corners. With so many getting sick, there was no one to do the washing.

"I found a village that still had some feverfew to spare, but we need more," Bors said. His shoulder slumped as he looked around.

Outside, the infirmary overflowed with patients. So many more had fallen sick in just one night. They filled every cot, and those who were not in real beds were in makeshift ones lining the chapel. Some were sitting up, but most were lying still, sweating in a death-like slumber.

The pages were spoon-feeding bitter feverfew tea to those who could still drink.

A chorus of moans could be heard from those in the grips of white fever. Nothing Father Walter was doing was working, and the sick showed no signs of improvement. Lancelot and Queen Guinevere were deep in fever. And with every loss, the old man seemed to lose more faith.

Galahad picked up the bag and looked inside, hoping for the best. But there was no sign of Cecily or Calib. He prayed they had found some other means of transportation to Poole. He hoped they would find Avalon.

"I have more bad news," Bors continued, lowering his voice to a whisper. "I took the coastal path on the way back to avoid any more thieves. And I spotted sails on the horizon. They bore Saxon colors. And they've begun *raiding*."

Galahad nearly dropped the bag. Camelot was too vulnerable to withstand an attack, even a small one.

"How far away?" He clutched the bag tightly to keep his hands from trembling.

"Three days at most. They were still far west when I saw them."

"Don't tell anyone else." Galahad grabbed the bottles of feverfew out of the bag. "We don't want people to panic. I will let King Arthur know."

"Time works against us," Bors warned. "We'll need to come up with something soon."

Galahad nodded and hurried to find King Arthur. The more he thought about it, the more his heart filled with dread. The timing seemed too perfect.

It was convenient that an unknown plague had arrived to Camelot shortly after a battle that had drained their supplies. It seemed convenient too that the sickness struck the strongest of Camelot first. Did the Saxons know about the sickness?

He was so lost in thought that he didn't notice at first that Red was standing guard outside the king's chambers. It was an unpleasant surprise, to say the least.

"Where did you get that?" Red asked, eyeing Galahad's handful of feverfew bottles. "I thought Father Walter said the medicine supplies were low."

Galahad couldn't admit he'd asked Bors to break quarantine. "I found some more hiding on one of the higher shelves."

Red looked at him, disbelief shading the plains of his face. His face was so like Arthur's, but different. Less lined, of course, but also lacking the smile that was quick to come to the king's eyes. Red smiled a lot, but never with a natural ease.

Galahad shrugged and tried to walk past into King Arthur's room. Red's arm suddenly blocked the doorway.

"What are you doing?" Galahad asked hotly. "I have an important message for King Arthur."

"No one is allowed in," Red replied solemnly. "The king fell ill this morning."

"The king?!" Galahad cried. "Why haven't you told Father Walter about this?"

Red rolled his eyes. "Isn't it clear that Father Walter no longer knows what he's doing? He's an old man whose forgetfulness is costing lives. We can't risk anyone getting sicker—especially the king. Anything you need to say to His Majesty, you can say to me, and I will relay it to him."

"And who put you in charge?" Galahad couldn't believe this was something the other knights could have agreed to. But then again, King Arthur had sent out his most trusted to seek more healers.

"I'm the only one of King Arthur's blood relatives still alive—closest kin. With Sir Lancelot and Queen Guinevere sick, the remaining knights have placed me in charge of his affairs. I'm the go-between."

The hair on Galahad's back rose. Something felt off about how Red had been put in charge so quickly.

"Now what is it that you needed to tell King Arthur?" Red asked.

"Just that I've found more feverfew," Galahad lied. Instinct told him that Red was not to be trusted. And while it was clear that Red didn't believe him, Galahad didn't care. He turned, but not before Red spoke.

"I get the sense that you don't like me, Galahad." Red stared at him, the expression on his face wolfish. "Why?"

"It's not that I *dislike* you," Galahad fumbled. "I just don't know you."

"Well," Red said, lightly tracing the pommel of his sword, "there's time to know me. Things have changed around here, and you should know . . ."

He trailed off, and though Galahad didn't want to encourage him, he had to ask. "Know what?"

"That I can be a very good friend . . . or a very bad enemy. The decision is up to you." Red opened Arthur's door and entered the king's room, locking Galahad on the outside.

CHAPTER 33

Calib woke up with a splash of fresh rainwater in the face and the late-afternoon sun in his eyes. His fur was still damp, but he was wrapped with a blanket, and the world around him was solid and still.

"Wh-what h-h-happened?" His teeth seemed to have taken on a life of their own as the cold overtook him.

Slowly, Cecily's worried face came into view. "You passed out," she said anxiously. She checked his pulse, but his pads were still so numb, he couldn't feel her paw on his.

"Captain Tristan?" he managed to wheeze out.

The sea rat's head poked in from the gathered crowd. Relief warmed Calib. The captain too was damp, but his coarse fur had protected him against the sea better than Calib's fluff.

Captain Tristan removed his hat and bowed. "You saved my life, and for that I owe you a great debt."

"It's all right, Cap'n," Calib mumbled. "No need."

"He accepts," Cecily said, and gave Calib a meaningful look that clearly meant: *Did you forget you lied to him about the Beast? You'll need this debt to save our hides!*

Calib pushed himself up and took a fresh blanket offered by Barnaby. Every muscle screamed in protest, but now he could see the damage around him.

There were cracks all along the deck from where a large piece of the masthead had split and rolled into the sea, taking the starboard guardrail with it.

The *Salty Pup* and her crew were sitting ducks, vulnerable to attack. Most of the sailors who Calib could see were helping repair what little of the guardrail remained.

"There's naught much that can be done now but let the ship drift along this northern current," Captain Tristan said, following Calib's gaze. "We will eventually near the coastline again."

"Will . . . we still be able to make it to Avalon?" Calib croaked out.

Captain Tristan nodded with excitement. "We're very nearly there, matey. That little bird we rescued is from Avalon."

"Num-nums for Karl?!"

Calib jumped, surprised. A lone baby seagull with curious eyes poked in above the group. A head taller than Calib, it was covered in downy gray-and-black feathers. A sling of burlap held its wing still at its side.

"Num-nums for Karl?" the bird repeated.

"His name is Karl," Captain Tristan said. He fished in his pockets and tossed a small anchovy to the bird. "That's about all he's told us . . . and that he's hungry."

"Num-nums!"

"How do you know he's from Avalon?" Calib asked as Cecily handed him a freshly brewed cup of tea. He took it gratefully.

"All creatures from Avalon bear the sign of the Silent Sisters," Tristan said, gesturing to the baby seagull's right claw. Calib leaned closer and saw a strange tattoo or birthmark: three swirls interlocked with one another. "The Manderlean had a similar one on his right ankle."

Calib started in surprise. "The Manderlean was from Avalon?"

Captain Tristan shrugged. "For a time, I think. He knew his way around the isle, that much is certain."

"And," Calib said, an idea, fragile as a moth, fluttered

at the edge of his mind. "You were able to land on Avalon *with* the Manderlean, but the second time . . . did the Manderlean come with you?"

"No," Tristan said. "What does this—"

"'But in the depths of the blackest sea,'" Calib interrupted, "'Only Avalon's mark will let you be'—that's it!"

"What's it?" Barnaby asked.

Calib grinned at his friends. "I know how to beat the Beast!"

"Hold up," Captain Tristan said, frowning. "I thought you said you knew—"

"Does it matter now?" Cecily asked, taking a step forward. "He just saved your life, Captain."

For once, the eloquent captain had no words. Tristan's mouth snapped shut, and though his face puckered, he didn't protest.

Calib grinned gleefully. "It's not about an *actual* mark that will get you past the beast—you have to be with someone who's *from* Avalon. You have to be a *guest* of the island . . . or else the Beast comes."

"How do you figure?" Barnaby asked, cocking his head.

But Captain Tristan had let out a cry of delight. "I see! When I first reached the shores, I was a guest of the Manderlean. The Beast did not rise. But the second time, that loathsome creature gave us the map and told us to go without him."

"And was this before or after your first attempt at the treasure?" Calib asked.

"After. Wait, you don't think . . ." Captain Tristan flicked his tail in annoyance. "The Manderlean was trying to get rid of me, wasn't he? He knew the Beast would come for me. He was hoping I wouldn't make it."

Calib nodded. "I think so.

Calib stoked the feathers above Karl's beak. "And now with this little fellow, you think we can reach Avalon?"

"We can try," Calib said.

"Avalon," Barnaby said, staring out at the horizon. "It sounds like a dream."

Captain Tristan observed the broken mast in distaste. "We'll just have to sit tight and hope the water brings up to whatever may come," he said.

"Whatever may come?!" Cecily shouted, incensed. "We need to get to Avalon as soon as we can! We have creatures counting on us!"

"Captain," a ferret crew member interrupted. "We have some complications to that plan of yours."

"What do you mean?" Captain Tristan asked.

The ferret pointed to the port side of the boat, away from all the repairs. In the waters, a long, lithe boat pulled up next to the *Salty Pup*.

It was painted blue, with a fearsome figurehead of a pine marten's skull against a black field: pirates!

CHAPTER 34

Wild yowls pierced the air as pirates rained down arrows onto the deck with metallic thuds. Everywhere Calib turned, large, brown pine martens were leaping over the railing and onto the ship. They wore patchy, mismatched armor, and helmets with long nose guards.

"Pirates to port!" Captain Tristan roared. He unsheathed his scimitar and ran to face the first of the pine martens swinging axes and spears. "Arm yourselves, mates!"

Pushing Karl in front of them, Calib and the rest of the

mice quickly ran for cover from the arrows. They ducked under an overturned dinghy.

"This is the unluckiest ship on the Seven Seas," Calib muttered. He was starting to wonder if something otherworldly was trying to keep them from finding Avalon.

"We fought against the Saxons; we can handle this!" Cecily said.

"Aye!" Barnaby agreed with such force that Calib looked at him in surprise. The storm seemed to have whipped courage into Barnaby. The brown mouse readied a slingshot.

Calib drew out his father's sword and breathed in deep. He hoped their string of bad luck would not extend to this battle. He motioned to Karl, who was roving around, trying to eat things.

"You stay put!" Calib instructed, pointing to the bird and then pointing to the ground. The bird took the hint and nodded.

On deck, the pirates pulled out the lighter barrels and packages, standing to form a line that led back to their raiding ship. They were here for the food, Calib realized, just like when the Darklings had been driven to desperate measures. Captain Tristan and his rats were trying their best to fend them off, but they needed help.

"Let's go!" Calib called, and sprinted into the fray, with Cecily and Barnaby only a moment behind.

The pine martens were fearless, with claws that lashed as sharp as swords. Captain Tristan's sailors were not used to paw-to-paw fighting, and the trained pirates were clearly winning.

"For Camelot!" the mice yelled together as they charged the line of raiding pine martens before they could take their supplies.

They had a few precious moments of surprise, but then the pine martens turned on them with angry ferocity. Barnaby stationed himself on top of a barrel while Cecily spun her blade in a constant figure eight, protecting them from any attacks.

Just when Calib thought that they might have a fighting chance to get to higher ground, there was a loud sound from a war horn. A bellowing voice echoed in the air.

"I have your captain!"

With horror, Calib saw the largest pine marten roaring in the middle of the deck. Spiked armor made from hedgehog quills ran the length of his back. A helmet made from a small, gold-plated kettle sat atop his head, and his big ears poked out from cracks along the sides.

And his paw was wrapped around Captain Tristan's throat.

"Surrender," the pine marten cried, "or else I will spill his life upon your deck!"

The battle stopped. Everyone's attention snapped to the two leaders.

"That's more like it," the pirate sneered. He turned to one of his crew. "Escort the captain to his quarters so we can negotiate terms of surrender."

"I don't negotiate with killers," seethed Captain Tristan, but a second later, he fell to the deck, gasping, as the pine marten punched him in the belly.

The pirate followed up with a cracking blow on Captain Tristan's jaw, which sent one tooth flying.

"You may call me Erik Blackwhisker," the pirate said. He walked over to the tooth and put it into his pocket. "And everyone negotiates with me, whether they like it or not."

"Well, we don't like it!" a voice called out from behind Calib. He knew that voice: it was Barnaby!

A moment later, a pebble arced over Calib's head and landed on the pirate's snout.

Erik's yellow eyes landed on Barnaby. "Why you—" He lunged toward Barnaby, and Calib saw with horror that his friend's slingshot was empty. Calib threw himself at the charging pine marten.

Bracing himself for an onslaught of brown fur and razor-sharp claws, Calib drew Darkslayer, prepared to die bravely like his father. He thought back to the tapestry back at Camelot, of Sir Trenton holding aloft the sword. He imagined this was how his father faced his own death—back straight, paws steady, and looking the enemy right in the eye.

But Erik Blackwhisker had stopped charging. Instead, he laughed, and the sound was more awful than Calib could have ever imagined.

With one swipe of his claw, the pine marten plucked Darkslayer out of Calib's paw. Erik held up the sword. It looked painfully small in his grasp, and Calib wondered how he could have been so foolish to think he could face a pirate pine marten.

Holding the blade up to the light, Erik let out a hiss of surprise. "What is your name?" he snapped at Calib.

Fear coursed thickly in his veins, but he straightened proudly.

"I am Calib Christopher, son of Sir Trenton Christopher," he proclaimed. The sound of his father's name made him no longer afraid.

Erik's eyes narrowed into golden slits. "This is your father's sword?"

"Yes," Calib said. "And he was braver than you will ever be!"

The pine marten howled an earsplitting shriek. He swung the large broadsword down on Calib's throat. Calib cringed and closed his eyes, bracing for the fatal blow, but the blade stopped short of making contact. He opened his eyes and looked around, half expecting to see his head separated from his body.

"If you are Sir Trenton's son, what was your mother's

name?" Erik's face was a mask, betraying no emotion.

"What?" Calib tried not to move with the blade just inches from the throat.

"Swear on your mother's name that you are who you say you are."

Calib swallowed and could feel the tip of his father's sword against his skin. "I swear on the name of Lady Clara Christopher—"

Erik dropped the sword from Calib's neck, and lunged forward again . . . and wrapped the mouse into a tight hug.

CHAPTER 35

Stunned, Calib stood perfectly still as the sharp claws grazed dangerously across his shoulders.

"They had a son! They had a son! Ahh ha-ha-ha!" Erik laughed until tears streamed down the corners of his eyes. He wiped them away.

Confused looks were on every face on the deck as they observed this abrupt change in the pirate king's demeanor. Erik paid them no mind as he sat Calib down on a nearby barrel.

"Now answer me this, why is his son with this sorry

lot? You should come be a pirate with me, I will show you the true seafaring way."

Calib shook his head as politely as he could, so as not to anger the volatile pine marten.

"Thank you for the generous offer. But I'm afraid—"

"Now whatever became of Trenton?" Erik asked, seemingly too excited to listen even as he asked for an answer. "What are you doing with his sword?"

"My father is dead many moons now. In an ambush by the Dark—"

Calib stopped short. He had told this story so many times growing up that he didn't even think twice about who the culprits had been behind his father's murder. But now the Darklings were his friends, and before that, Merlin in wolf form had claimed that the Darklings were *not* the ones responsible for Sir Trenton's death. Only, Howell never got a chance to tell him who actually *was*.

"Sir Trenton was killed by the dark?" Erik asked, confused.

"In an ambush," Calib finished, correcting himself. "We never knew who did it."

"And your mother?"

"Dead of sea fever a few months after that."

Erik shook his head sadly, placing a paw over his heart.

"Terrible shame; she was a fine mouse. What about

Sir Owen and that sniveling fellow, what's his name . . . Sir Perry."

Calib scrunched up his nose. "Sir Perry? I don't know any Perry."

Erik waved his paw impatiently. "He was a vole with breath worse than a seagull's."

A hot flash of anger filled Calib as he realized the pirate must be referring to Sir Percival Vole. Onetime friend of Camelot and his father, and now cowardly traitor.

"Owen is dead as well," Calib said. "Killed this last autumn, betrayed by Sir Percival."

Erik scowled, his features crumpling into a painful grimace. He covered his face with his paws. Calib thought the big pine marten might be mourning for his father.

"How did you know all these mice from Camelot?" Calib asked, reaching out to offer comfort.

Erik jerked away and hissed. "That tricky fur-beast! Trenton spared my life on the high seas, when he had every chance to slay me. But instead, he made me promise to owe him a favor, that he could call upon me one day to pay it back."

The fur on Erik's neck rose. "He put me in his debt, and then he goes off and dies on me? His wife too?"

Calib wondered how many places his father had traveled and how many creatures' lives he had changed. Even to this day, his father's actions continued to echo into

Calib's own like little water ripples from a fallen pebble. Even this strange pirate knew of him and his friends.

"Now I will forever remain in a ghost's debt, and I cannot abide that!" Erik growled as he paced on deck at an impatient lope.

"You could . . . pay back your debt to his son by freeing us," Captain Tristan suggested, his sailors loyally surrounding him.

Erik paced the deck, the quills in his armor clacking together. After long seconds, he stopped.

The ugly rat speaks some truth," the pine marten proclaimed. "I'll let Sir Trenton's spawn go. But the deal is a life for a life—and that doesn't count for your little mousey friends nor for this captain and crew."

"No!" Calib shouted. "You must release them!" But he could see by the flare of the pine marten's nostrils that he had pushed Erik's mercy too far.

"You forget who is in charge," the pine marten snarled.

Calib tried another approach. "Why did my father spare you?"

"His men ambushed us during one of our raids," Erik said. "I challenged him to a duel to the death instead. Winner kept his head and the loot, but when he bested me, he spared my life, regardless."

"We want a similar deal," Calib said quickly. An idea formed in his mind. He knew that he could never best the pine marten, but there were other ways. . . .

"I need this ship and its creatures to complete my mission," Calib continued. "So we challenge you to a duel!"

Calib made eye contact with Cecily just then. His best friend gave him a quizzical look before realizing what he intended to do. She nodded slightly.

"No." Erik shook his head. "I won't duel with a Christopher again. Took me years to live that down."

"You misunderstand," Calib said, trying to keep the excitement clear from his voice. "You'd duel with our best fighter . . . Cecily von Mandrake!"

He pointed at Cecily, and she gave a small bow to the pine marten.

"That little whip of a girl mouse? You're pulling my tail," Erik said, the fur on his back raised in indignation.

"She's faster than any pine marten I know," Calib proclaimed. "It took three to subdue her."

Erik's guards looked at one another sheepishly. "She was fast," one of them admitted.

"Don't believe me? Duel me and find out!" Cecily challenged.

All of Erik's claws were out now, fully extended. "That would be an unfair fight," he said.

"For you, maybe." Calib crossed his arms. "If she wins, you must let everyone on the ship go."

"You have no bargaining rights here," Erik hissed.

"Then perhaps you are too afraid to offer the same chance my father offered you. Or . . ." Calib took his time, preparing for the set up. "Perhaps you fear being bested by a mouse-maid."

He held his breath, hoping he hadn't pushed the pirate too far again. The pine marten would either fight and then kill them, or just kill them all now.

"Very well," Erik Blackwhisker finally said, fangs gleaming. "We duel."

CHAPTER 36

Cecily tied the ends of her whiskers together behind her head.

"The first thing they teach you in the kitchen is how to keep your whiskers from singeing," she said quietly to Calib as Erik sharpened his blade. "The same principle applies in a duel. I have no interest in resembling Sir Owen, rest his soul."

Calib remembered how sensitive their former combat trainer had been about his one remaining whisker. The others had been lost to a ferret in a duel, but Sir Owen always kept his last remaining one oiled and shining.

A pang of sadness spasmed in Calib's chest at the memory of the old black mouse.

Cecily took out her sword, a nimble fencing sword fashioned from a Two-Legger needle. Weighing it for balance, she practiced a few attack moves. Calib backed up to avoid its sharp point.

"Erik underestimates us. I'll use that to my advantage," she said, lightly carving a *C* into the railing. "Now wish me luck!"

Calib's tongue seemed to be sealed to the top of his mouth. This wasn't training anymore. If Cecily lost, the price would be high. Too high.

"Cecily, are you sure you want to do this?" he asked. "We can think of something else."

"Just wish me luck!"

"G'luck," he managed softly. But that still didn't seem like enough.

"I'm sorry for taking all the credit for our adventures and for the Harvest Tournament," Calib said, forcing himself to meet Cecily's eyes. "I just wanted to be what everyone else thought I was: a hero my grandfather could be proud of. Instead, I let my pride get ahead of me. Forgive me?"

Cecily gave a few practice thrusts. "You were a puffed-up pigeon for a while there"—she slashed a quick figure eight—"but you're my best friend, Calib. Of course I forgive you."

She lowered her sword and smiled at him. "And next time, I'll just give you a little prod with my rapier and deflate you a bit."

Calib grinned back. "Deal."

Cecily sheathed her weapon. "And thank you."

"For what?

"For trusting me to see us through," she said. And with that, Cecily marched to the center of the deck.

A large crowd of pirates and prisoners had gathered. As Calib slipped next to Barnaby, he observed Erik, who was practicing with an ax in each paw. Just one of them looked like it would take two mice to lift. Calib wanted to cover his eyes with his paws. What had he gotten Cecily into? He was glad Karl was safely away in the captain's room. This was no sight for a young bird's eyes.

Captain Tristan stepped forward. "The duel concludes when one opponent has dealt the other an irrecoverable blow," he announced. "What irrecoverable means . . . well, that is up to their opponent.

"On my count. Three . . . two . . . one!"

Erik and Cecily circled each other, sizing up each other's speed and stance. Everyone grew silent as the two picked up their pace, racing each other to keep the opponent on the opposite side of the circle.

Suddenly, Erik lunged toward Cecily, hissing as he

swung an ax up from his waist, nearly clipping Cecily on the snout.

Barnaby let out a squeak as the crowd around them roared. Calib stepped forward to help Cecily, but Captain Tristan lay a stern paw on his shoulder.

"She's on her own in this," he whispered.

As Erik tried to swing his ax back down on Cecily, she jumped out of the way. Again and again, Erik lunged across the circle with his weapons swinging. But Cecily kept dodging them. The pirate grew more flustered with each attempt to catch his quarry.

"This is a coward's approach!" Erik shouted, winded and heaving. "Stop running and face me like a real fighter."

Finally, the pine marten charged with all his speed and slammed an ax down. Wood splinters went flying, nearly taking out a nearby rat's eye.

The head of Erik's ax had lodged firmly into the higher deck.

In the few seconds Erik needed to pull his weapon out, Cecily sprinted. She leaped onto the pine marten's back and delivered three swift blows to the back of his neck with the hilt of her sword.

Erik crumpled with a loud thud.

The stunned crowd stared at the unconscious pirate leader before Captain Tristan shouted triumphantly, "He's down!"

Two pirates grabbed Cecily from behind. Swords were drawn again.

"You've tricked us," one of them growled.

"Fair's fair! Cecily is the better swordsmouse!" Calib yelled. "You were the ones who attacked us first; how's that for fair?"

Erik stirred. "We raid to survive. Our home, Vikeland, bears little crop," the pine marten said. Some of his lieutenants rushed over to help their leader sit up.

"So you just take it from others and destroy their homes?" Calib asked, his paws clenched into fists. "We saw what you did to the villages south of here!"

"That was not us," Erik spat on the deck. He looked like he was waking up with a pounding headache. "Those animals were led by a creature with a golden mask—the very same villains who forced us off our homeland of Vikeland. He left a trail of destruction and blamed it on us."

Calib and Captain Tristan looked at each other, the same fearful recognition flickering in their eyes.

"If the Manderlean and his Saxons are already openly attacking the British coast," Calib said, "that means he's probably headed back for Camelot again. We have to go back and warn them."

"We can't go back without a cure!" Cecily protested. "We need to get to Avalon as soon as we can. Maman could be . . ." Cecily didn't finish the sentence. She didn't have to.

Calib was torn.

"We have two ships," Barnaby pointed out.

"Aye," Captain Tristan said. "But the *Salty Pup* is dead in the water without the mast."

Calib turned to Erik, channeling his desperation into something like bravery. "The Saxons won't stop until *we* stop *them*. We must defend *our* home. You understand that, right?"

Erik was silent. His eyes flicked from Calib, to Cecily, to Barnaby, and back to Calib, where they finally rested on Darkslayer's hilt.

"We will concede a small lifeboat for your journey to Avalon," Erik said, sitting up and holding a paw at the back of his neck.

"But, Erik," one pirate protested, "they will say we are weak!"

"They will say that we were fair and merciful," Erik corrected. "And that is not a bad thing to be, considering the times ahead."

Captain Tristan shook his head. "That lifeboat won't fit us all. With that hungry bird, only one other creature will fit. And as captain, I claim that spot for myself!"

"You're wrong," Calib said flatly. "It might fit just one gull and one selfish sea rat, but it could also fit one gull and two small mice."

"I've traveled too far to turn back from Avalon!" Tristan raged. "I'm too close to the treasure!"

Barnaby coughed. "Excuse me, Captain? But I think you're forgetting something: Calib saved you twice now. You owe him a life debt."

Tristan opened his mouth to protest, but Erik leered at him, twirling his ax deftly with his paw.

Tristan sighed. "Take that Avalon bird and be off. I know when the odds are against me."

"Trust me, better to pay off these life debts as soon as you can." Erik nodded at Tristan. "The *Salty Pup*'s crew may come aboard the *Snowreaver.* Just know, I plan to the turn the sea red with Saxon blood before the day is out."

Captain Tristan brushed a paw across his scar. "Aye. I too have a score to settle in that regard." He turned and barked orders to his sea rats.

Erik looked down at the Camelot mice with what Calib thought might be a hint of admiration.

"Go, then, son of Trenton," the pirate said softly. "Forge your own oaths."

CHAPTER 37

The moon was high in the night when Red finally departed King Arthur's room. The boy locked King Arthur's chamber door every night and set two sentry men to guard it.

Galahad peered from around the corner, gauging the guards' alertness. It was hard to tell if they were there to keep people out . . . or King Arthur in.

But with a little help from a plant called nightfoil, Galahad knew that they would be asleep soon. He'd slipped the sleeping powder into their drinks at dinner, and it was only a matter of time before the guards' heads dipped down into sleep.

When the last guard finally shut his eyes, Galahad quickly stepped inside and shook Arthur awake.

The king did not stir.

Arthur's breathing was ragged. Galahad checked his pulse. It was there, steady, but slow. Very, very slow. Carefully, he propped up the king.

"Galahad?" King Arthur murmured as he shifted to waking. "What's happening?" A coughing fit interrupted the king. The dry rattle scraped across Galahad's ears. It was worse than he had thought.

"Hello, Your Majesty," he said quietly. "I came to make sure you were all right. Red won't let anyone—even healers—in."

But the king didn't seem to hear him. He was lost in his own feverish dreams. "I used to think the Saxons were our biggest threat, but I see fire. Animals of sizes and colors and the wailing . . ." Pain spasmed across Arthur's face. "A plague will ravage us faster than any army. I should have hired more healers. . . ."

Another round of coughs racked King Arthur. Galahad patted King Arthur's back until his body stopped shaking.

"Thank goodness for Red, at least," he said. "Why the expression, young du Lac?"

Galahad only faintly registered the king's question as he

stared at the empty mudberry bottle on the bedside table. Mudberry—a small amount could numb a fever, but an entire bottle . . . an entire bottle could kill a king.

Hands shaking, Galahad picked it up. The white fever didn't come with a dry cough—it was marked by headaches and fevers. Mudberry poison, on the other hand, trickled down to the lungs, slowly suffocating its victim.

He knew he hadn't liked Red from the moment the boy had shown up; he was a show-off and a busybody. But never had Galahad suspected that he would be capable of *poisoning* King Arthur.

And yet, here was a mudberry bottle, completely empty. He slipped it into his pocket to show Father Walter. The old healer would know what to do.

"Don't worry, Your Majesty," he said, "I can fix this. We just need to get you out of here."

Laying Excalibur on the ground, Galahad pulled the half-conscious king off the bed and across his shoulders. It took all his strength to keep them balanced.

King Arthur nodded weakly. His eyes fluttered closed, and he leaned back onto his pillows. His brow knitted in pain.

"Come on, Your Highness," Galahad pleaded. "You need to get up."

At that moment, the door burst open. Red marched into the room with two guards.

"Seize him!" Red shouted. The guards obediently stepped forward.

Galahad's gut instincts took over. He quickly kicked his treasured sword deep under the bed and grabbed King Arthur's magic-less one. He brandished Arthur's sword as his own at Red and his retinue, but he knew before even beginning that this was a lost cause.

"Why?" Galahad asked, trying to buy time. "What crime have I committed?"

"Attempted regicide," Red exclaimed. He pointed again. "Arrest Galahad du Lac for trying to kill the king!"

CHAPTER 38

As soon as Calib stepped into the pirates' rickety dinghy, he deeply regretted it. Climbing down the rope ladder had been terrifying, and now he had to steer this little lifeboat all the way to Avalon?

"Lifeboat my paw," he muttered under his breath. "*Death*boat is more like it."

The boat rocked wildly with every small wave, banging against the sides of both the *Salty Pup* and *Snowreaver*, Erik's pirate ship. Their only means of steering were two thin reed oars.

Karl, whose wing had been re-slung in a fresh cheesecloth, made rowing even more difficult with his excitement. He swung his neck from side to side, taking everything in and making the boat rock.

Barnaby's head popped up over the railing of *Snowreaver.*

"Take care!" he called as he waved to Calib and Cecily. "I'll make sure I get everyone to Camelot safely!" The brown mouse would accompany Erik, Captain Tristan, and their crews in an attempt to cut off the Saxon fleet.

Again, Calib marveled at Barnaby's newfound confidence. Barnaby had grown in the time they'd been on this sea journey. He was no longer the meek first year parrying with his eyes closed. Now he was learning how to look over navigation charts with Captain Tristan and had eagerly told Calib and Cecily that Erik had promised to teach him the pirates' language from the Northern Lands. Calib had grinned at his friend's glee, and realized with a pang that he'd underestimated Barnaby entirely. He wouldn't do that again.

Captain Tristan appeared next to Barnaby on the deck of *Snowreaver.*

"Avalon is due west, toward uncharted waters," Captain Tristan said. "Use the setting sun to guide you, and the North Star after that. You should arrive before nightfall. I would not want to be on the water after dark."

"Why's that?" Calib asked, though he was afraid of the answer.

"The Beast of Avalon sleeps during the day." Captain Tristan suppressed his shudder. "If you're wrong about the meaning of your poem, well . . . your best chance of eluding him will be during daylight."

Mouth dry, Calib could only nod.

"Just promise me one thing," Tristan said, lips set in a thin line. "If you find whatever the Manderlean wanted on Avalon—destroy it. Whatever it is, it can only bring about great devastation. Better it never fall in any paw than have it fall in his."

Calib looked into Tristan's eyes and saw a glint that was warmer and brighter than the gleam of gold: the kindness of a recent stranger to a new friend.

"On my honor," Calib said, "I will."

"And on mine," Cecily added.

As Erik untied the rope and let it drop into the boat, Cecily and Calib each took an oar. Turning their back to Karl, they began to row in unison.

Calib watched *Snowreaver* slowly disappear from view until it was a tiny speck in the distance. With each pull of the oar, he felt less and less sure of his plan.

"Num! Num! Num!" Karl chanted to keep them on beat. They continued like this as the sun rose high above them. It shone down with a blinding, stifling heat. Calib squinted to keep his sweat from stinging his eyes. Soon, he was panting from the effort.

After a while, Calib and Cecily began to take turns with both oars so that the other could get some rest. Karl had given up on his chanting. His head tucked under his unbroken wing as he slept.

Eventually, a current picked them up, and both were able to break. Exhausted, Calib and Cecily shared the last of their water.

"That was incredible what you did back there, fighting against Erik," Calib said. "You saved us all."

"It helped that you believed in me," Cecily said, smiling.

"It's just . . . I knew I couldn't do it myself," Calib admitted. "Everyone thinks I'm so great after the Battle of the Bear, but it was really Berwin and King Arthur who turned the tide against the Saxons. I'm just benefiting from other creatures' brave deeds, like yours. I can't even make squire by myself."

"Calib, is that what you think?" She put her canteen down. "You sell yourself short."

"No, everyone's sold me too tall— Er, you know what I mean." Calib's ears drooped as he felt the weight of his confession fill the air. "I'm not like my father or grandfather at all. I'm sorry I tried to take your victories to make up for it."

He felt relieved to get all this off this chest, finally. But now that it was out in the open, the awkwardness of his confession floated around him like a bad smell.

Cecily looked at Calib for a long while, until Calib squirmed under his fur.

"I don't know when you're going to realize," Cecily finally said, sounding exasperated, "your strength is not to be the best at *everything,* but to be the best *you* can be."

Cecily picked up the oars. "I don't know any other mouse in Camelot who tries as hard to fight for what is good and right. That's what being a true knight is all about."

Calib let Cecily's words sink in. It seemed almost too simple. And what if one's best wasn't enough . . . ?

After a few hours of traveling, the sun began to set like a glowing egg yolk over the horizon. Karl stirred from his sleep and squinted ahead.

"Karl! Karl!" He hopped up and down with glee. The mice leaned forward to see what the bird was yammering about.

"Look! I see it!" Cecily exclaimed. A thin gray strip of land was illuminated against the sun.

"Oh, thank Merlin!" Calib said, leaning back in relief.

Ker-SPLASH!

"Karl!" Cecily cried. With dismay, Calib realized the excited seagull had thrown himself over the side of the rowboat.

"Karl! Karl! Karl!" Karl squawked as he floated in the

water, beating his one good wing in an attempt to take off for his home.

"Get back in the boat, Karl!" Calib said. "Come on, we're taking you there."

Suddenly, something thumped the bottom of the boat. They rocked wildly, and Calib dug in his claws.

"What was that?!" Cecily exclaimed.

Out of the corner of Calib's eye, he saw a ripple of water heading for the boat. A ripple that could be made only by something very big.

"The mark of Avalon is no longer with us," he said, voice tight. "The Beast doesn't think we're guests anymore." He cupped a paw around his mouth and yelled, "Karl, come back!"

A barnacle-covered tentacle surged out of the water!

"The Beast!" Cecily gasped as the tentacle wrapped around the boat and crushed it into splinters. Calib had just enough time to suck in a gulp of air before he plunged into the ocean again.

"Cecily! Karl!" he choked out, trying to keep his head above water. A wave splashed over him, causing him to splutter.

"I'm fine!" Cecily shouted. She had grabbed ahold of some passing debris and used it keep afloat. "Find something to float with!"

"No num-num! No num-num!" Karl bobbed in the water. He flapped hard, but could not take to the air with his useless wing.

Calib's stomach lurched as he saw a giant shadow slide underneath them.

Something looped around his footpaw and squeezed tight. In an instant, Calib was jerked underwater.

Try as he might, he could not kick free. He struggled to grasp his sword, but it got tangled in his wet cloak. With the last of his breath, he looked down at the black, writhing mass of a giant sea monster.

CHAPTER 39

The creature opened its mouth, and a deadly sharp beak protruded forth, snapping. Calib tried to scream, but only bubbles came out. Salt water poured into his mouth and burned his throat. It reminded him of the briny fish stew Madame von Mandrake had made three Harvest Tournaments ago, though the Emerald Sea's water wasn't nearly as delicious.

Funny, Calib thought, *what your mind thinks about before you die.*

The giant squid clutched him tighter. He hoped Cecily

and Karl were all right. Cecily would take care of the bird, and he knew she would reach Avalon, find the cure, and save Camelot. As he watched the surface of the water retreat farther away with each second, Calib faced his own end with disappointment. Was this how the Christopher legacy would end—in the cold, unwelcomed depths of the ocean?

Suddenly, a blur of white feathers streaked past him. Then another and another.

Seagulls!

The sound of their cries echoed underwater like a slow siren's call. The birds pecked the creature's fleshy head. The beast flinched. For a moment, the tentacle tightened so hard around Calib that he thought he might pass out . . . and then the tentacle released him.

Immediately, he began to kick for light and air. He was out of breath, though, and his strokes were weak. . . .

Something slammed hard beneath Calib, and suddenly, he was ricocheting toward the surface. He looked down to see an olive-colored shell beneath him. He was on the back of a sea turtle!

He and the turtle exploded to the surface with a spray of water. Calib wiped the salt water from his eyes and glanced around.

Two gulls bobbed in the air next to him. Cecily sat on her own sea turtle, looking just as surprised as he was.

She nodded her head at the back of the seagull's right leg. Each of the birds bore the same tattoo, a trio of swirling patterns.

These were both creatures of Avalon.

"Are we near the island?" he asked eagerly, whiskers twitching with excitement. But his smile faded at the seagulls' cold glares.

"Not so fast, matey," the turtle beneath him intoned in a deep, mellow voice. "We didn't rescue you out of the goodness of our hearts."

"You didn't?" Calib asked, his joy deflating.

"We came to rescue my son!" A third seagull, large with gray wings, landed on the turtle's back. She wore a red sash across her chest, marking her as the leader of her flock.

"Hello, General Alva," said the turtle. "There's no sign of your son, but we've captured his kidnappers."

"His kidnappers?!" Cecily cried. "We were bringing him back home to you!"

General Alva's tail feathers ruffled angrily. "Our scouts saw you— He had his wing tied up."

"We set his wing because it was broken," Calib explained.

"You mean you *broke* his wing!" she shrieked like a harpy. Her beak snapped out, as if she was ready to snip Calib's ears off. "I knew the Manderlean would try to use our own against us, but this is monstrous behavior!"

"No, it was broken in the storm. We *rescued* him!" Calib said. "We're not with the Manderlean at all; we're from Camelot!"

"Then *where* is my son?" General Alva said, her words punctuated by frustrated squawking.

"I don't know." Calib's ears drooped. "We lost him when the sea monster surfaced."

"Serves you right for rowing right into its clutches," General Alva said, voice still full of anger, but her eyes scanned the water anxiously. "If I don't find my son, alive and well, I will feed you back to the Beast myself."

Calib's paw fell to his sword hilt, ready to defend himself if that was the case.

"Ma! Ma!"

Everyone turned to see Karl flying over with the aid of two seagull cadets. He landed with a thud on the turtle's back and hopped to his mother.

One of the cadets bobbed his head in a seagull salute. "We found him floating west of here. He keeps asking about two mice friends."

"You can understand him?" Cecily asked as Karl hopped over to her, nearly knocking her down in his effort to nuzzle her.

General Alva gave Karl a gentle peck on the head. "And it serves *you* right for wandering away from the flock during a storm," she chided, but there were happy tears in her eyes.

Karl chattered for a moment, a smattering of squawks that Calib couldn't quite understand, though he could catch small mentions of "Cawwib."

General Alva turned to Cecily and Calib.

"Normally," she said, "I would require a feather before granting an audience, according to the Code of Wings."

Calib nodded, understanding all too well. In order for bird leaders to grant an audience with someone from another species, they first must be presented a feather from their own kind. Last time Calib attempted to adhere to the Code of Wings in order to talk with the owls, he had nearly lost his tail.

"But as you have brought me a whole bird—my son, no less—I will grant you a favor. What are your names?"

"I'm Calib Christopher of Camelot," Calib said.

"And I'm Cecily von Mandrake, also of Camelot," Cecily curtsied, even though her soaked skirt clung to her legs. "We seek the healers of Avalon."

"Camelot." The general tilted her head and studied them. "The Lady of the Lake has been expecting you."

Calib looked at the gull in surprise. "But how—"

"How does the Lady do anything?" Alva cut in. "Magic. Come, Calib and Cecily of Camelot, I'll fly you there." She lowered her neck to let the mice scramble up to settle on top of her shoulders. "Grip tightly to my sash and try not to move too much."

Calib and Cecily had flown on owls before, but seagulls were smaller. Plus, they flew much higher than owls ever did. Calib found that he tolerated the flight much better if he looked ahead instead of down.

As they soared across the great expanse of blue sea, the island grew closer. A hazy fog clung to its mountain peaks like a thick sweater. The last light of twilight illuminated only the silhouettes of sharp, jagged mountain peaks and dark evergreen trees poking above the mist. Soon, the moon rose like a solitary candle from the east.

"There she is," Alva whispered. "A more beautiful island ne'er existed."

"Why all the secrecy?" Cecily asked, leaning forward toward the general's ear. "Why is Avalon hidden from the rest of the world?"

"Magic bleeds from this world like a wound," General Alva replied. "And the Two-Leggers have become too greedy for it. The island protects what little is left. That is why the only way to get onto this island is to accompany someone who is from it."

"Well, we don't want any magic," Calib said. "We just want a cure for Camelot."

"From what I've heard of Camelot's plague, it may be magic that you need."

A familiar tingle ran down Calib's spine. What did she mean?

They were passing the first mountain range. Over the razor-thin ridges, Calib could see a large crater in the middle of the island, with blue water sitting at the bottom of it.

The lake glowed a mystical blue, producing its own light, much like the light that Calib had seen permeating through Merlin's Cave.

An eerie sense of déjà vu crept over him. "I've seen this before," he said.

"They say a great star fell from the sky in the Old Days and turned the earth it touched into a magical wellspring," Alva said as she descended to the ground in a long spiral. "Some of that exposed star is buried here, and the magical waters that came from it sit in this lake."

"It's beautiful," Cecily whispered.

"Another note of warning for first-time visitors," General Alva said. "The Lady of the Lake's patience is limited. Don't ask too many questions, and when you do ask a question, make sure it is the right one."

Calib furrowed his brow. He had so many questions! He wanted to know the truth about his father. Who had actually killed him? And the answer to Kensington's question in the wisdom challenge, which would let him finally become a squire. But those were selfish questions. Nothing compared to the greatest one of all: how could they save Camelot?

"Thank you for the warning," Cecily said. "Is there anything else we should know?"

"Yes." The general banked hard. "Do not lie. The Lady of the Lake can see right through that, and she will not appreciate it."

Alva landed at the very edge of the glowing lake. The wispy mist that gave the mountains their mysterious aura was thick here. Calib drew a deep breath and tasted something spicy in the air like cloves and cinnamon.

"Good luck," Alva said as Cecily slid off to join Calib at the edge of a glassy lake. "Thank you again for saving my son. I shall return after your time with the Lady of the Lake is over."

"Are you not coming with us?" Calib asked.

Alva shook her head. "The Lady comes only to those who have need, and with my son returned to me, I have none."

They waved good-bye as Alva took off into the sky, and Calib was surprised to feel sorrow at the bird's departure. Her presence was comforting and strong, like he imagined his own mother's would be.

"Who do you suppose we're looking for? A Two-Legger?

A cat?" Cecily asked, peering out into the middle of the lake. Calib breathed deeply again, enchanted by the flowery, spicy smell. It made his tongue feel numb and his fur tingly.

"Hello!" he called. "We're two travelers from Camelot. We seek the Lady of the Lake!"

His voice echoed across the lake, but only silence answered back.

Cecily tried. "There are many sick at Camelot," she called. "The whole castle is vulnerable to an attack from the Manderlean and his Saxons!"

Nothing happened.

"Maybe we have to say something special to summon her?" Cecily said in a normal voice.

Calib thought about Dandelion's song. They had gotten past Avalon's beast. Was there a step in there they'd forgotten?

"We've come from very far to seek your aid! We've bested the sea monster!" Cecily tried again.

Still nothing.

Frustration took hold of Calib. He snatched a pebble from the banks and threw it as far as he could. It skipped three times.

"It's a matter of life and death! In the name of Merlin, I implore you!" Calib shouted.

A light wind began to blow, and the fog dispersed.

"All matters deal with life or death" came a whispery voice, carried on the mist.

Emerging from the fog, a snowy-white egret approached, gliding smoothly on the translucent water.

CHAPTER 40

As the white egret stepped onto the shore, she stretched out her neck to full height, a length longer than three mice standing nose tip to tail.

Calib backed up with his jaw falling open. The egret was the most fascinating bird he'd ever seen. Everything about her was long and lean. Her thin legs unfolded like branches as she stood, making her even taller. Her sharp beak stretched at least five inches to a deadly point.

"Greetings, Calib Christopher and Cecily von Mandrake," she said. "I am the Lady of the Lake."

"How is it that you know our names?" Cecily asked.

"I have seen it in the water," the Lady of the Lake said. "I also know what you seek. I've been waiting for someone from Camelot to come, but I had thought it would be a Two-Legger. The boy called Galahad."

"He stayed behind to help the sick," Calib said.

"Then the boy denies his destiny and his duty," the egret said, sounding frustrated. "I suppose that's what you get when you rely on humans."

"What do you mean?" Cecily asked.

"The sword the boy carries has power," she said. "Power to rebalance our world, rid it of evil . . . or in the wrong hands, rid it of good."

Calib's mind reeled. He knew, of course, that Excalibur was magic, but not that so much depended on it. "Merlin never mentioned what the sword could do."

The Lady of the Lake eyed Calib shrewdly, looking into his eyes as though she could see all his secrets and fears. General Alva was right; he could not hide anything from her piercing eyes.

The egret blinked, then nodded knowingly. "I see you've also met Myrddin," the Lady of the Lake said, turning to preen her feathers. "Tell me, is he still gallivanting about as a wolf? A more foolish being, I've never met."

"Merlin wasn't foolish," Calib said, feeling defensive of his friend. "He was the greatest wizard who ever lived!

He gave the last of his magic to help us save Camelot."

"And tell me, how is Camelot faring these days, hm?" the Lady of the Lake asked. "Not well, I presume, or else you wouldn't be here."

"You're right." Calib looked down at his paws, feeling hot in the face. "A terrible disease has taken hold."

"Disease? No, it's no disease." The Lady of the Lake looked at them like they were terrible students. "It is a curse."

A curse! Calib didn't think curses still existed in the world, that they only belonged to tall tales told by Madame von Mandrake. His eyes widened as Cecily gasped beside him.

"Where did it come from—and how can we break this curse?" Cecily cried.

The egret closed her eyes. "A spell this strong . . . We believe it is fueled by a corrupted piece of magic, tied to a broken-off piece from Merlin's treasures."

Calib's stomach somersaulted. Legend spoke of three treasures that Merlin had entrusted to the animals. The owls were gifted Merlin's Crystal, which had helped Calib unlock Excalibur from the stone. Merlin's Mirror, with its prophetic powers, had been given to the Darklings, but that was rumored to have been smashed during the Great War between Camelot and the Darklings.

There was supposed to be a third treasure entrusted to

the mice of Camelot. But none among the mice had ever seen the thing or knew what it was. Most assumed it was the castle itself.

"Which treasure? What does a corrupted piece of magic look like? And—and *who* would curse Camelot?" The questions fell out of Calib's mouth like a waterfall. Cecily elbowed him in the ribs and mouthed the word "one!"

The Lady of the Lake's black eyes flashed with annoyance.

"There is only one person powerful enough to accomplish such a deed—a disgraced sister of Avalon who turned against her own kind and began practicing black magic, a magic that left trees dead and creatures cold in her wake: Morgan le Fay!"

Calib remembered the story Madame von Mandrake told of the inn's elm that had been blackened by a sea witch. He pulled his tail closer around him, as though it could keep away the growing chill.

"Maman's story," Cecily said under her breath as she came to the same conclusion. "The witch could have been Morgan le Fay!"

The Lady of the Lake nodded her head sadly, her head swooping in graceful arcs. "Merlin was the first to recognize the magical talent in King Arthur's half sister. He insisted that she be trained, but Morgan was driven by jealousy of her younger brother. She began to practice dark arts, growing too strong for any one of us to challenge her. At great cost, our spies confirmed that she had obtained a fragment of Merlin's treasure. It now seems clear what she intended to do with it."

"We saw Merlin's Crystal before. It was still whole when it became part of Excalibur. So she must have corrupted a piece of Merlin's Mirror," Calib said, fitting the pieces together like a puzzle.

"Or a bit of the third treasure," Cecily said. "We don't know anything about that one."

The Lady arched her neck, staring at the stars reflected in the lake. "I have been combing the waters time and time again to try to find the answers, but the water turns against us every time. Observe."

She brought her long beak down onto the water.

"In aqua, verum," the egret said. She brought her long beak down onto the water, but as soon as she touched the surface, the lake turned an inky black. Quickly, the lady snapped back up, sending droplets into the air as she shook her head. "Something blocks our vision."

Calib tapped his paw nervously on Darkslayer's pommel. "But surely you and the Sisters are powerful enough," he said. "That's why we're here: we need Avalon's magic to help save everyone!"

"Let me tell you a little something about magic, little

beast." The Lady of the Lake moved in close to their faces. Her beak a mere centimeter from Calib's face. Her voice no longer kind but cold and domineering. "Once you give them a little taste, then all they want is more, more, more! Merlin should never have meddled in the affairs of men. Now he's upset the balance in a way that could mean the ruin of us all."

"What do you mean," Calib whispered, "'he upset the balance'?"

"The world of men has become too strong," the Lady said, her voice rolling like thunder across the water. "Their ways are destroying our magic. It is only the natural order of things that they should fall, as other empires have fallen. Only then will we return to the Old Days. So why try to fight off the inevitable? If it wasn't the Saxons or disease, there would be something else that ends Camelot."

"You don't mean that," Cecily said, and Calib was surprised to hear a sob in her voice. "King Arthur and his knights brought peace to the land! They are a force for good. You don't want to help because you are too selfish with your magic!"

The Lady of the Lake stood up and spread her wings. Cecily and Calib took an instinctive step backward. The wings were impossibly large and seemed to swallow up the sky around them. The egret could smack Calib across the water as easily as a skipping stone if she wanted. He winced, bracing himself for whatever came next, but the Lady only stared down at them stoically.

"Camelot is already doomed. Before I lost sight of the castle, I saw its downfall. Don't believe me? Look for yourself!"

Cautiously, Calib tiptoed to the edge of the water. He peered down, but all he could see was his blurry, wavering reflection.

"What am I supposed to see?" he asked.

"The lake requires a gift of great value," the egret explained. "It gives as much as you give."

Calib and Cecily looked at what they had brought with them. It wasn't much. They had left nearly everything on the ship. The only thing Calib owned that was of any worth was his father's sword, Darkslayer.

"You don't have to do this, Calib," Cecily said quietly, correctly guessing what he was thinking. "Your sword is the only thing connecting you to your father and grandfather."

Calib caressed the hilt with his paw. It was true, this might be the most important reminder of the Christopher legacy. But then again, he knew what his grandfather Yvers and father, Trenton, would have done in his situation. It wasn't even a question. He couldn't spend all his time thinking about the past when the future was at stake.

"The present matters more," he said.

Calib threw the sword away from him as hard and as far as he could. He did it quickly, so he wouldn't have time to think about or regret it. The sword fell into the lake with a splash, and the water glowed more blue.

"Very good, the lake accepts your offer, for it was of much value to you," the Lady of the Lake said. "You now must submerge your head *into* the water and open your eyes."

"How do I know what I'm looking for?" Calib said. "I'm no seer."

"But you have a connection to the Two-Legger boy," the Lady of the Lake said.

"Galahad? What does he have to do with it?"

"He was supposed to be here so that I may finish his training with Excalibur," the egret said sadly. "I believe he is now in great danger, untrained and unaware of the power he holds in his hands. Perhaps you can find out what has happened to him."

Calib nodded, then crouched down. He sucked in a big gulp of air and plunged his face underwater.

CHAPTER 41

The lake was surprisingly warm, and parted with ease, as if he were coated in oil. When Calib opened his eyes, it did not sting like he imagined.

At first, all he could see were drifting pieces of seaweed. But after a moment, the seaweed began to blur, until it formed the shape of the castle. Calib felt a strange vertigo, a sensation of floating midair above the moat. He looked below him at two torches lighting their way to the shore.

As he focused on the scene, he saw Mistress Pearl and two of her troubadours lowering a funeral boat into the water. The pages had all gathered around it, each laying down a gift into the boat to accompany the dead into the Fields Beyond. Two field mice, both Darklings, wept, clutching each other for comfort.

Calib's insides felt uncorked. He floated closer and saw Edwin's body lying in a small reed boat. He swallowed a cry, feeling responsible. He hadn't been able to save him in time.

Then Calib watched as Macie stepped up to the boat. Her fur was stringy and limp, like she'd been sweating. Just as she placed her gift, she collapsed on her knees. Calib reached out instinctively to touch her.

Suddenly, something seemed to grab Calib by the neck and jerk him forward. He flew toward the castle at lightning speed, until he thought he would crash against the stone walls.

Calib opened his mouth to scream, but to his surprise, he sank right through the stonework and into Goldenwood Hall.

He was astounded to see the arena filled with rows of makeshift cots and beds. Cries of suffering rent the stuffy air. Calib's stomach turned a little queasy. He was surrounded by sick and dying animals.

The force then yanked him through King Arthur's chambers. There, the king and Galahad stood, the former leaning on the latter. They were surrounded by armed guards with their swords out. One of them stood behind Galahad and raised the butt of his sword, about to bring it down on Galahad's head.

"Watch out!" Calib shouted out.

He accidentally gulped in a mouthful of water and pulled his head out from the lake, choking and gasping for air. Cecily caught him as he fell back onto the shore.

"Everyone's in danger! Almost all are sick!" Calib said as soon as he'd coughed out the last of the water. "King Arthur, Sir Lancelot, the queen . . . and Edwin . . . He's . . ." He clutched his sides, his wet fur chilling him to the bones.

"Maman! Did you see my mother?" Cecily asked, her paws clutching his tightly.

Calib shook his head sadly. He recounted to them everything that he'd seen. Finally, he looked up at the Lady, who had stood as quietly as the long reeds that danced in the night air.

"Help us lift this curse," Calib pleaded. *"Please."*

"Haven't you been listening to anything I've said?" the Lady of the Lake said. She flapped her wings once, hard. The wind knocked Calib and Cecily onto their tails. "The downfall of Camelot is inevitable."

"But the Sisters of Avalon trained Morgan!" Cecily pointed out. "This is your fault as much as it is Merlin's!"

The Lady of the Lady grew quiet. She turned to face

away from them. Her eyes cast downward to the lake.

"Morgan le Fay was my brightest human student. Brilliant, ambitious," the Lady whispered. "But she coveted magic, which is what drove her to evil. I don't know which treasure of Merlin's she corrupted, but it would have appeared in your castle a few days before the sickness began."

Calib tried to remember if Saffron was carrying anything with her when she arrived to the castle. But nothing came to mind.

"To break the curse, you must find the piece that Morgan has corrupted and destroy it with the sword, Excalibur," the Lady of the Lake said. "But knowing her cleverness, she will have disguised it as something else."

Calib's calm crumbled. "Then it could be anything!" he cried.

It would take them at least a week to make it back to Camelot. If things had gotten this bad on their way here, who knew how much worse the situation could be by the time they returned? The image of Edwin, so small in his boat, haunted him. Calib shut his eyes and wished the memory away.

"How will we get back to Camelot in time?" he whispered into his footpaws.

"I will grant you one last favor," the Lady of the Lake said, a touch of guilt in her voice. "But you must swear an oath to stop the one they call Manderlean once and for all."

"What's the Manderlean to you?" Cecily said, her voice raw. "You've already made it clear that you don't care what happens to us."

"I suspect Morgan is connected to this creature somehow," the egret said. "Do you wish to return to Camelot the easier way or not?"

"We do, and we promise to defeat the Manderlean," Calib said, giving Cecily a warning look. He needed the egret to get them back to Camelot, and they would do well not to interrogate the Lady of the Lake when she had a boon to give.

The Lady of the Lake swung one wing over to the lake. "Take one sip from the lake, and it shall send you back to Camelot."

They followed the egret's instructions and scooped a pawful of the water.

"Drink," the Lady ordered, "and think of a place near Camelot that won't alert Morgan's senses."

Calib caught on at once. "Howell's crystal cave."

They sipped the water while clutching paws. A fizzing sensation filled Calib's veins.

He squinted back at the Lady of the Lake. To his amazement, he could see the outline of a ghostly Two-Legger woman with silver hair, dressed in white robes, surrounding the egret.

"What are you?" he tried to ask, but the liquid traveled down Calib's throat like ice, freezing and melting and freezing again. A mist came over his eyes, and the world started to glow at the edges of his vision until everything was swallowed up in blinding light.

"Remember your promise to Avalon!" he thought he heard the Lady of the Lake say before her voice faded into a faraway distance. He squeezed Cecily's paw tightly, and the world spun around them in a blue-and-silver swirl.

CHAPTER 42

Feeling dizzy, Calib closed his eyes. He couldn't even feel Cecily's paw in his. The only sure thing in the blur of the lake's magic was his own heartbeat. He focused on it, and for a moment, it seemed as though it was speaking to him in Howell's voice: *Remember your legacy.*

Eventually, the sensation slowed down, and he opened his eyes. Calib was staring at the opening of the tunnel at the rocky shoals along the bottom of the castle. The moon hung over them, and Calib recognized it as a full one—a wolf moon.

"Thank you, Merlin," he whispered.

Cecily and Calib raced through the tunnel, running uphill all the way.

"We find Galahad first, then Commander Kensington and Maman," Cecily said, her mouth set in a thin line.

"Where is everybody?" Calib said as they made their way through the Two-Legger kitchen. The castle was too quiet. The halls were deserted, of Two-Leggers and animals both. Normally, night was the prime time for the mice to replenish their own stores from the Two-Legger scraps.

They sprinted to Galahad's chambers, but instead of locating the boy, they were shocked to find two of Mistress Pearl's troubadours riffling through Galahad's things. The entire room had been ransacked. Galahad's clothes were dumped on the floor, and his books torn from page to page.

Cecily looked around, aghast at the mess. "What are they doing here?" she demanded in a whisper. Calib winced— He'd forgotten that he'd never told her about the letter he wrote for Mistress Pearl. A prickly guilt tickled his spine as he looked at the overturned room.

A troubadour finally noticed them. "Ah, the mousy who let us into the castle!" He grinned, a grotesque sight as one of his front canines was black with rot. "You've come back sooner than expected."

"What are you doing here?" Cecily asked again. Her drawn sword quivered, not as though she was scared, but as if she was barely holding herself back from setting upon them.

"Easy there," said the other troubadour, the one wearing a jester's shoes and a jingle-bell hat. "Pearl asked us to look for something."

"Where is the boy who lives here?" Calib asked.

The troubadour shrugged lazily. "No idea. Not here."

"Did Commander Kensington say you could do this?" Calib pressed. He tried to stay calm, though his instincts were clamoring at him that something was not right. He reached for Darkslayer's hilt. . . . Too late, he remembered he had thrown the sword into the lake. He was unarmed.

The troubadours looked at each other. "You'll have to talk to Mistress Pearl about that," one said. "She speaks for Kensington now."

"Then where is Mistress Pearl?" Cecily demanded. "I've had enough of your excuses!"

"She's looking for—"

"The cure!" finished a new voice in the room.

Mistress Pearl stepped in wearing a full nurse's garb, a white face mask covering her snout. "I'm looking for the cure, as it seems you, Calib Christopher, came home empty-handed."

Calib felt a wave of relief upon seeing the powerful healer.

"Actually," he said as he hurried over to greet her, "we made it to Avalon and spoke with the Lady of the Lake. She says the white fever is not a sickness at all, but a curse caused by a corrupted piece of Merlin's treasure!"

Mistress Pearl blinked once above her mask. Then twice. "That explains many things then—and only makes it more necessary that my troubadours continue the search. I need something to amplify my own powers. Healing one dead tree is much less difficult than healing an entire castle." She looked at Calib, and he saw that the fortune-teller appeared exhausted. Her paws trembled, and the charcoal that rimmed her eyes only highlighted how bloodshot they had become.

"It will be all right," Calib said sympathetically. "Thank you for your help. Now, please, do you know where everyone is? We need to find Gal— Er, the commander."

"I've had to enforce a strict curfew and quarantine rules to keep the disease from spreading," Mistress Pearl said, leaning against the wall. "It's safer this way."

"Did Commander Kensington agree to this curfew?" Cecily asked, eyes narrowing. Calib noticed Cecily had not yet sheathed her sword.

"My dear," Mistress Pearl said, sounding infinitely weary, "when we arrived, your commander was close to death herself. It was only by my powers that she still clings to life in the sickroom. No one is allowed in, and I would not risk you."

She sank onto one of Galahad's socks that had been displaced by the troubadours' riffling. "I was hoping that the Two-Legger with the magic sword would have something to assist with my healing, but it seems he does not."

"You really should ask permission first, before going through his stuff," Calib said.

"Permission from a Two-Legger?" Mistress Pearl said, sounding scandalized. "You two must be very tired from your journey. Why don't you get some rest, and we will discuss it further in the morning."

"But we have no time to lose!" Cecily all but shouted. "We need to find the cursed treasure."

Mistress Pearl waggled her paw. "Now, now, I won't take no for an answer. Are you the healer or am I?" She wearily got to her feet. "We need to get a good night's rest before we start any search parties." Turning, she addressed her two troubadours. "Snout, Quince, please escort the mouslings to their rooms."

Cecily opened her mouth the protest, but Calib shot her a warning look. She hesitated, then allowed the troubadours to take them to the dorms. Calib pretended to close the boys' dorm door behind him, but just as quickly snuck back out and over to the girls' room.

"Thank Merlin, you're back!" Devrin said as Calib entered the room. She scooped Calib into a bone-crushing hug, then she held him out at arm's length. "Where's Barnaby?"

"He should be back in a few days," Calib said, straightening a whisker that had gotten extra crumpled in the reunion. "And he'll be bringing some of our new friends."

"Cecily said it was you who sent that awful Mistress Peal to us," Dandelion said. "Did you really?" The young mouse was looking forlorn from her bed across from Devrin's.

"She knows how to heal," Calib said defensively to Devrin. "Hasn't she been helping?"

Devrin snorted. "Hard to tell. She's turned the castle upside down looking for medical supplies. She's put us all to work trying to find Merlin's old things in the cellars."

"And she won't let me visit Ma and Pa. I haven't heard from them in a whole week," Dandelion added, her whiskers trembling. The field mouse's fur was rumpled, and her eyes were bloodshot. The loss of her best friend, Edwin, must have been hard on her.

"Mistress Pearl is convinced the cure can be found among Merlin's things," Devrin added. "Ever since you left, the sickness has spread even more quickly. Nearly all the adults are sick now."

"Hold on," Cecily said. "Just the adults?"

"Warren's the only page. There was Saffron and Edwin, too, but . . ." Devrin glanced at Dandelion. The young mouse had buried her head in her paws.

Cecily patted the Darkling's shoulder while Cecily's snout crumpled in a way that let Calib know her mind was working at top speed.

"What are you thinking?" he asked, breaking the sad silence.

"That it's odd," Cecily replied. "Usually, a sickness takes the youngest and oldest first."

"It's not a plague," Calib reminded her. "It's a curse. Why couldn't the curse be crafted to take out the strongest and most experienced of Camelot first? What if the curse was *aimed* at the adults?"

"Yes," Cecily said, "but that doesn't explain why Edwin and Warren got sick, then . . ."

Devrin looked between them, eyes wide. "A *curse*?"

"We've been to Avalon and learned a lot of things," Calib said. Quickly, he explained everything while Dandelion and Devrin listened with rapt attention.

"So now we have to find a cursed piece of Merlin's treasure and destroy it with Excalibur," Calib finished. "Do you know where Galahad is?"

Devrin's whiskers trembled. "Galahad's been arrested for kidnapping and trying to kill King Arthur," she said.

Calib felt as though the world had been pulled from

beneath his feet. "That's absurd!"

"It is," Devrin said solemnly. "But his trial is at dawn, and Red has said that justice will be immediate."

"We need a plan!" Calib cried. "We need Galahad and Excalibur to save the castle!"

Devrin and Dandelion exchanged glances.

"Actually," Devrin said. "We had an idea."

CHAPTER 43

"Today begins the trial of Galahad du Lac, who now stands accused of plotting to murder the king and erstwhile bring harm to Camelot," Sir Kay, King Arthur's foster brother and former castle steward, proclaimed in the throne room.

Galahad flinched at the accusations. This was wrong. All wrong.

It was *Red* who should be put on trial.

Red who was responsible.

Red who was poisoning the king.

As Sir Kay droned on about the logistics of the proceedings, Galahad scanned the half-empty room. Most of the castle's residents were now too ill to attend, and the faces who were there were new, recently hired by Red. They all had mean, sallow looks about them.

He glanced toward his fellow pages, who had shown up in solidarity for him. Bors glared at Red, but he was not powerful enough to help Galahad.

"You are charged with trying to kill our king," Sir Kay snapped at Galahad. "If I were you, I'd pay better attention, seeing as your life depends on it."

Sir Kay seemed to take pleasure in Galahad being put through this indignity. After the Battle of the Bear, King Arthur had reprimanded Sir Kay and given his title of keeper to Galahad's father, Lancelot. Ever since then, Sir Kay's dislike of Galahad had gone from secret to glaringly obvious.

Galahad straightened up, his hand lightly trailing over the sword on his hip. He could do this.

"I call upon Red," Sir Kay said. "He will provide a firsthand account of the assassination attempt."

"Thank you," Red said, standing up. His hair gleamed copper in the golden light, and he'd changed into the royal colors. He looked princely, except for the smug expression on his face. "I walked in and saw Galahad with his sword poised over King Arthur."

He paused as the crowd murmured. Smirking, he raised his voice and continued. "I heard Galahad say that there could be only one of them with a magical sword."

Red held up a small glass jar. "Once I subdued the prisoner, I found this jar of mudberry poison in his pocket." He paused again, allowing the information to sink into the courtiers' minds. Whirling dramatically, he pointed at Galahad. "The king isn't sick from the plague—Galahad's been poisoning him!"

Angry jeers filled the room, but one voice rose above the rest.

"Bring King Arthur forward to speak!" Bors shouted. "Where have you been hiding our king and queen? Who are these soldiers you've brought in without his permission?"

"Why are you wasting our time?" Malcolm added. "What about the Saxons? There have been reports of coastal raiding!"

Red glared down at Bors and Malcolm, and Galahad was proud of his friends for not taking a step back.

"With the king and queen ill, *Uncle* Arthur put me in charge, since I'm his closest blood," Red snarled. "The castle has been left undefended with so many sick, so I had no choice but to hire more men."

Again, he pointed at Galahad. "King Arthur is close to death thanks to this page's actions. He is too ill to testify.

It is my *right* to speak on the king's behalf."

Red marched up to Sir Kay and removed the gavel from the older knight's hand. He turned to face the hall. "With the authority of the crown, Galahad du Lac, I hereby proclaim that you are *banished* from Camelot!"

A rumble of shock rumbled through the gathered crowd, and Sir Kay pounded his goblet on the Round Table to get everyone to quiet down.

"But the crown may be merciful," Red said, standing up. "I will ease the sentence under one condition."

Galahad's mouth was dry, but he forced himself to speak. "What condition?"

Red smiled his sly smile. "That you give up Excalibur."

CHAPTER 44

From the safety of a mousehole positioned right above the Round Table, Calib swallowed back a cry of outrage. How dare Red propose such a thing! Excalibur belonged to Galahad, and Galahad alone.

Galahad's face paled at Red's proposition, and Calib watched as the boy's hands grasped the sword's hilt. To the mouse's horror, he then saw Galahad slowly let go and unbuckle his sword belt. He was going to give up Excalibur!

Calib turned to face the handful of mice gathered

behind him. Cecily and Dandelion had rounded up every mouse who was still healthy enough to move—all of them pages. It wasn't a large group, but it would have to do.

"Rub it along your teeth," Devrin said as she finished handing out thistles dipped in a last bit of cream from the mice's stores.

"No biting," Dandelion reminded. "Just scare the Two-Leggers enough to get them moving out the doors."

Calib turned back to look at the stained-glass window behind the throne. "Any time, now." His muscles tensed with adrenaline. Suddenly, a black wing waved up and down outside a missing panel.

"For Camelot!" Calib shouted, leading the mice through the hole and into the open.

They sprinted straight for Galahad. Those around the Round Table jumped up in alarm. Shouts and shrieks filled the air as Two-Leggers sprang out of their seats to avoid the rodents rushing across their expensive shoes.

Sir Kay's voice could be heard the loudest over the din. "Rats! There are rabid rats everywhere! They must be spreading the plague!"

Calib ducked and dodged the stampeding feet around him, narrowly avoiding Red as the boy tried to stomp on his tail.

"Everyone, stay calm!" Red yelled, unsheathing his blade. "They're just mice!"

A large rock suddenly smashed through the stained glass behind the throne, raining rainbow-colored shards onto the mayhem. Behind it, a flurry of black feathers followed.

An entire battalion of Valentina's crows swooped into the room, snatching hats, pecking at heads.

"For Camelot!" Devrin yelled from Valentina's back. She jabbed at the Two-Leggers beneath them with her sword.

"The animals have gone mad!" Sir Kay yelled. With arms over his head, he followed the stampeding crowd out the door.

Only Red stood his ground, slashing at the ground and sky. His eyes were fixed on Excalibur. Calib knew—knew with all the fur on his back—that Red would never let Galahad leave the hall with the sword.

Suddenly, Red looked down at his pockets. He reached in and withdrew a struggling creature.

"Dandelion, no!" Calib cried as he watched the boy throw the calico mouse against a wall. She crumpled to the floor.

"I've got her!" Devrin called from Valentina's back. "Just get Galahad out of here!"

A moment later, Devrin somersaulted onto the ground, scooping up the unconscious mouse just before Red reached them. Delivering a nasty gash to Red's outstretched hand,

Devrin pulled Dandelion into the nearest mousehole.

Calib turned his attention back to Galahad. The guards on either side of him were busy fending off an onslaught of crows. Seeing the opportunity, Galahad shoved into them.

"Follow me!" Calib said, arriving at Galahad's feet.

"What?" Galahad said, looking dazed. "When did you get back? Did you get the cure?"

"Come on!" Calib said, pushing Galahad's shoe. Why wasn't Galahad doing what he said? It was almost as though the boy didn't understand him, though his hand was on Excalibur's hilt. He shoved once more against Galahad's boot, and then took off, hoping the boy had gotten the hint.

He had. Galahad sprinted after him and through the window, careful to avoid the broken glass. Queen Guinevere's garden lay on the other side. They splashed across the pond, thickly choked with algae. Calib jumped onto the low stone wall separating them from a plummet into the sea.

"Wait!" Galahad cried, skidding to a stop. "There's no way out from here. Arthur destroyed the steps ages ago to prevent a seaside attack." He gestured to the sheer rock face that dropped down some twenty feet to a crumbling set of narrow stairs that looked nearly indistinguishable from the cliff.

Calib gasped for breath as he climbed onto the wall, praying that Cecily had been able to get the next and most crucial part of the plan into place.

Reaching the top of the wall, he looked down.

"Hello, young Christopher!" a tawny owl hooted from a flock that circled right below the top of the wall.

"Hello, General Gaius! And hello to your brigade!" Calib called, grinning. He turned and looked up at Galahad. "We have a way down."

CHAPTER 45

"You, um, can't really be telling me to jump and be caught by the owls . . . right?" Galahad asked

The mouse nodded, squeaking in urgent bursts.

Galahad shook his head, feeling Calib's words falling meaningless on his ears.

"I'm sorry, I don't understand."

The mouse got louder, clearly frustrated with Galahad's slowness. He dashed at the sword at Galahad's side. Suddenly, the mouse froze. He glared at Galahad accusingly.

"You're right," Galahad whispered. "It's not Excalibur—it's King Arthur's sword. They are an exact match. *Twins.* When I heard Red's footsteps, I switched them. Red knows that King Arthur's sword is no longer magical, so I thought that the safest place to hide Excalibur would be right under Red's nose."

Calib's ears drooped, then he quickly used his tail to scribble some letters in the sand: S-W-A-R-D = K-U-R-E.

"Excalibur can cure the sickness?" Galahad asked. Hope rose in his chest as the mouse nodded. Galahad tapped the hilt of King Arthur's sword again, wishing more than ever that it was his faithful Excalibur.

Galahad leaned out again. Just below the lip of the cliff, he could see the owls moving into position. Ten or so flew in a semicircle. They held a fisherman's net aloft with their talons.

"I don't know if you've noticed," Galahad said, a queasy feeling in his stomach. "But I'm a lot heavier than you." He spared another look at the mind-boggling distance between where they stood and the rocky shoals below. If the fall didn't kill them, a sharp rock would.

Calib also looked uneasily at the net, but at that moment, there was a cry from the broken window. Red's mercenaries had spotted them. The desperation to get away jolted Galahad into action. Saying a lightning-fast prayer, the boy grabbed Calib and jumped.

For a breathless moment, Galahad wondered if he had just doomed himself. There was enough time to think about his father, who lay sick in the infirmary, and his mother, Lady Elaine. What would she do when she learned her son was dead and accused of attempting to assassinate the king?

But before he had an answer, he landed in the net with more force than the owls seemed to expect. For a moment, he thought the owls would manage to hold him up, but then they began to descend with alarming speed.

They were falling!

A large tawny owl screeched to the others. It wore a long red sash that flapped in the wind. At their leader's command, the owls rallied, and the speed of their descent slowed. The sensation of falling left Galahad light-headed, but at least they weren't plummeting to their deaths.

They landed on the large flat rock with a hard thud. Stars sprang across Galahad's eyes, as he hit the rock squarely on his side. There would definitely be bruises later.

The owl came to rest on a nearby rock, his chest puffing up and down.

"Thank you . . . ," Galahad said, trying to find the right way to express his gratitude to his animal rescuers. He slowly stood up, then bowed deeply to the owl.

Looking pleased, the owl returned the bow.

Another mouse, the same one who'd been with Calib to collect the feverfew leaves, ran up to them from behind the rocks. They said something to the owl leader, and with a wave of his wing, the owl and his fellow birds took to the sky once more, banking south in a V formation.

Galahad followed their flight path with their eyes before turning to face the castle, which was now several thousand feet above him. Excalibur was in there . . . and so was Red. If Red got a hold of the sword, who knew what he would be capable of doing.

"I need to get back to King Arthur's room," Galahad said to Calib. "I'll need to sneak back up through the secret tunnel."

The mouse squeaked something that sounded like a protest.

"I know a secret way into Arthur's chambers from the cellars," Galahad reassured him. "Will you come with me?"

He was surprised when Calib shook his head. Again, Calib's tail scratched an image into the dirt: a circle with four lines.

"The Round Table? You want me to meet you there?"

The mouse nodded, then drew a symbol of the sun, which Galahad guessed meant noon.

Galahad wondered what Calib was up to, but he trusted

his furry friend completely. "Deal," he said, extending his index finger for Calib to shake.

Calib clutched it with both his paws, and with a handshake, the two friends parted ways.

CHAPTER 46

Valentina flew Calib and Cecily back to Guinevere's garden. Crawling between two stone blocks where the mortar had fallen away, they entered the throne room, then snuck through the mousehole that led to the Goldenwood Throne. This was the meeting point for all the pages after they had cleared the throne room and rescued Galahad.

There were a few injured here and there, but Cecily and Devrin were attending to them. Calib spied Dandelion nearby. She had a bandage wrapped around her head and was resting comfortably in a hammock made out of an old sock.

The young mouse looked up with guilt in her eyes. Her whiskers drooped, and she possessed none of the perkiness she had before. Calib paused. As annoying as she usually was, this version of Dandelion was far worse.

"How are you feeling, Dandelion?" Calib asked.

"Devrin says I have a concussion. She gave me something to keep my head from swelling," she said. "I didn't mess up your plan, did I?"

Calib gave her an encouraging smile. "You did great, Dandelion. Why, you went straight for the worst villain of them all!"

"Well, he *was* the one responsible for Edwin getting sick, wasn't he?" she said, her voice thick with unshed tears.

Calib looked at her in surprise. "What do you mean by that?"

Dandelion struggled to sit up straighter. "Well, you said the Lady of the Lake told you the corrupted piece of magic probably entered the castle a few days before everyone got sick. And from what I overheard in the Two-Legger kitchens, *Red* arrived a few days before— I'm sure he brought all kinds of stuff to the castle."

Calib sat back on his heels. The Darkling page was right!

"Well done, Dandelion!" he said, patting her paws. "Clever!"

Dandelion's ears turned to pink. "It's nothing," she mumbled. "I've just been thinking of Edwin a lot. . . ." Though her words were quiet, there was also a rocky determination underneath them. Calib remembered how Dandelion had tended to Edwin when he was sick.

Calib stood up. "We need to search Red's room. Now."

Devrin poked her head up from bandaging a page's paw that had been stepped on. "According to the moat otters, Red's search party just left Camelot to look for Galahad along the cliffs."

"Let's go," he said, "while we still have a chance."

"I want to come," Dandelion said, clambering up from her hammock.

"You're injured," Devrin protested. "You'll need days of rest!"

"I feel fine. Plus, you need me."

"And why's that?" Devrin said, hands on hips.

"Because I've already stolen this key from his pocket," Dandelion said. She withdrew a metal key she had tucked behind her.

Even Cecily looked impressed.

Red's room was in the remotest tower in the castle. And as Dandelion slipped the key into the lock, Calib discovered how the boy had used the room's location to its full advantage.

Red's room was cluttered with books and scrolls, all of them stolen from the library just a floor below.

Stacks of them lay askew on the ground. Every record of Camelot's history prior to King Arthur had been squirreled away here. On Red's desk, a large scroll lay open. Calib looked over the spidery writing:

I had brought with me the three treasures of Avalon in the hope that with their power, we could introduce an age of peace among men unlike any before.

"He was reading all of Merlin's old records," Calib said, looking up into the uneasy eyes of his friends. "Translating them."

"There's a lot in here," Cecily said grimly. "We better get started."

An hour later, they were still sifting through piles in Red's trunk. Calib was tired, hot, and starting to feel very hungry.

"It would help if we knew what we were looking for," Dandelion muttered.

"If the piece of corrupted magic is from the mirror, it would be glass, I think," Cecily said.

"But we don't know what the third treasure is," Devrin said grumpily. "It could be anything."

As Calib pawed through the finely stitched tunics and

britches, it occurred to him that everything Red owned was newly made or barely worn. All his clothing was done in Arthur's colors of Pendragon blue and gold.

"Edwin would have been better at this than me," Dandelion said, whiskers trembling. She tried unsuccessfully to dig under the mattress. "He had a particular talent for combing through Two-Legger things."

Calib could hear the emptiness in Dandelion's voice when she spoke her friend's name.

"Dandelion, I've been thinking," he said, "and I think *you* should have the wooden circlet. Edwin made it after all, and I'm sure it will help you remember him."

Dandelion smiled faintly. "It's pretty silly, isn't it? I told Edwin you wouldn't like it," she said. "Even so, it wouldn't be half as good if Edwin *had* made it. He was the worst at wood carving."

"What do you mean?" Calib asked, a nagging sensation biting his chest. "I thought he said he carved it himself. . . ."

"He just wanted to impress you. Edwin actually traded for that," Dandelion said, shaking out one of Red's clean handkerchiefs, then setting it aside. "He got it from a traveling bard who stopped by the day before the strength challenge. Edwin exchanged some lavender-scented oil for it."

She wrinkled her nose. "It was the best trade ever, too. The bard smelled awful—like rotten eggs."

Something twisted in Calib's gut like a sharpened knife. "What did you say?" he asked.

Dandelion repeated herself, but Calib's mind was already racing. He'd only met one other creature who seemed to exude such a sulfery smell. And he was the last creature Calib wanted back at Camelot: Sir Percival Vole.

Calib bolted toward the door.

"Hey! Where are you going?" Dandelion asked.

"Tell Devrin to take everyone and meet back at Goldenwood Hall," Calib called over his shoulder. He crawled back into the floorboards and began to step quicker. As the dread gripped his insides, he began to run.

What if that *ring* was the corrupted piece of Merlin's treasure?

But it didn't make sense, exactly, because Calib wasn't sick. Though, now that he thought about it, he had never *directly* touched the ring, never worn it. He'd been wearing the leather gloves for the strength challenge. Who had touched the good luck crown?

An image of Warren grabbing the crown and putting it on his head popped into his mind. Warren was the only page to have fallen ill. . . .

And Edwin, who'd knelt as he'd presented the ring, was now dead.

But Saffron, his mind whispered. She never touched the ring.

Anguish filled Calib. But she *had* told him that everyone in her village touched the fortune-teller's wooden circlet. A wooden circlet that had sat on top of her cloak's hood.

Reaching his dorm, Calib dashed to the foot of his bed and threw his chest open. He quickly pulled on his leather gloves and rummaged through his trunk. . . .

But the wooden circlet was gone.

CHAPTER 47

The sound of tiptoeing paws and jingle bells made Calib whip around. One of Mistress Pearl's troubadours, Snout, was sneaking out from behind the dormitory curtain where he'd been hiding and was now near the door.

In his gloved paws was the cursed Two-Legger ring.

"Hey! Give that back!" Calib shouted, and the troubadour dashed toward the door. Outrage lent Calib a surge of speed he didn't know he possessed. He charged the traveler and delivered the hardest kick he could manage at the animal's knees.

Caught off balance, the ferret's legs buckled. He stumbled back with the cursed ring. Trying to recover, he swung it down on Calib's head.

The mouse rolled away before it could make contact, and sprang to his feet. He was weaponless. Desperately, he looked around the room for something—anything—to use. But he was too slow. The ferret was out the door!

Calib tore after him, but the distance between them was growing. The troubadour was too fast.

Suddenly, Mistress Pearl and Cecily appeared at the other end of the hall.

"Stop him!" Calib shouted. "He has it! The curse!"

Quick as lightning, Cecily tripped the ferret. The ring fell from his paws and skittered across the floor. But before Calib could reach them, Mistress Pearl pulled a knife from her robes and drove it straight through the ferret's heart.

Calib and Cecily cried out in shock. The ferret looked with surprise into Pearl's makeup-smudged face.

"But . . . ," he managed just as Mistress Pearl drove the knife even deeper. The ferret's eyes glazed over, and his head slumped forward.

"Why did you kill him?!" Cecily shouted, her voice shaking. "You didn't have to kill him! We had him!"

"This was one of Morgan le Fay's spies," Mistress

Pearl said grimly. "He deserved what he got. And he betrayed me."

She wiped her knife clean with distaste. "He came in here on *my word* that we would bring no trouble to Camelot, and here he is, causing the biggest trouble you could have imagined! I had to make things right by you."

Calib shook his head, trying to clear his mind. His grandfather would never have killed someone like that, and neither would Kensington. Camelot prided itself on giving everyone a fair trial. He wasn't sure he agreed with Mistress Pearl, but there was no time to think on that now.

Carefully, he scooped up the ring with his gloves. "This is the missing piece."

Cecily took a step back from Calib's outstretch paw. "We need to get it to Galahad immediately," she said, looking queasy. "The Lady said Excalibur can break its curse."

Led by Calib, the animals rushed back to the agreed meeting point of Goldenwood Hall. It was easier to get there than Calib had expected, as Red's soldiers were still away from the castle, searching for Galahad. For once, things were going their way.

But as they darted through the makeshift infirmary of Goldenwood Hall and rounded the last mouse tunnel bend into the dim light under the Round Table, Calib felt his hope suddenly extinguished.

A Two-Legger boy was in the throne room, but it wasn't Galahad.

It was Red.

CHAPTER 48

Galahad sprinted down the stairs from King Arthur's chamber to the throne room. His muscles cramped into a tense knot. It had taken him longer than he expected to sneak into King Arthur's room. And when he arrived, the true Excalibur was already gone—along with King Arthur.

He had the very bad feeling that Red was two steps ahead of him. He unsheathed King Arthur's magic-less sword. It was better than nothing.

As he arrived at the throne room to meet the mice, he

heard voices carrying through the door. He paused, hiding behind a suit of armor in the hallway.

"Thinks that he can run and hide? I'll find him. And it won't go so easily for him. There will be no trial this time."

Moving as quietly as he could, Galahad approached the double doors that led inside. He could see Red pacing back and forth behind a seated old man. The man's eyes were closed, a crown perched crookedly on his head.

With shock, Galahad realized that it was King Arthur. His face was as pale as parchment, and he looked twenty years older than when Galahad had seen him last.

"It's my right!" Red continued, almost shouting now. He seemed to be talking to Arthur, but the king showed no sign that he could hear. Red grabbed Arthur's quill from the center of the table and shoved it into the king's hands. "Now sign the execution order."

And as the boy turned, Galahad saw something that made him feel like the floor had suddenly disappeared and he was falling into Camelot's cellars.

Excalibur hung at Red's hip.

Red gave the king's chair a shove, and Arthur leaned precariously to the side. "Come on, old man! Sign!"

Anger filled Galahad's veins. Not only had this boy stolen what rightfully belonged to Galahad, but he was treating their king—the man who had served Britain for years—no better than a dog.

"You want me, Red?" Galahad shouted as he slammed the double doors open. "Then come and get me yourself."

Red paled but quickly recovered his usual demeanor. A smile crept across his face.

"You came back. I'm impressed. But I suppose I shouldn't expect less of Lancelot's son. You are earnest to a fault. Now hand over Excalibur."

Galahad lowered his blade a fraction. Red had not yet realized that he *was* holding Excalibur and that the sword in Galahad's hand was King Arthur's magic-less blade.

"You've already got one magic sword," Galahad said slowly, trying not to stare at Excalibur and hoping his mind would catch up. "Are you starting a collection?"

"You know that King Arthur's sword is worthless," Red said. He was not smiling anymore. He drew Excalibur, the metal rasping softly against the leather scabbard. He held its edge to King Arthur's throat.

"Give up Excalibur, or Arthur dies."

Galahad stood still, trying to look like he was considering Red's offer. If he said yes right away, Red would realize that he had been tricked.

Red pressed the blade harder to Arthur's neck. A soft groan escaped the king's lips, but he did not open his eyes.

"All right! You win," Galahad said, trying to force disappointment into his voice as he lowered King Arthur's sword. Gently, he placed it on the Round Table. It truly was a twin to Excalibur in every way. Even the markings along the blade looked the same.

"Now," Red said, "back away from the sword."

Galahad considered many options—including grabbing Arthur's sword from the table and attacking—but Red could still reach the king before he could. The older boy had every advantage.

His eyes never leaving Red's, Galahad took a step backward. Then another. As he took a third step, he noticed a small movement around Red's feet. He continued backing away until he felt stone wall against his back.

"Stay right there," Red ordered, and moved toward the table to claim King Arthur's sword. As Red reached for the hilt, Galahad saw a tan mouse with a white patch on his left ear scamper away from Red and dart underneath the table.

A confused expression came over Red's face. The boy took several awkward hops, then pitched forward onto the flagstones, Excalibur and Arthur's sword clattering to the floor.

Calib had knotted the laces of Red's boots together!

Galahad would have laughed if the circumstances weren't so dangerous. He ran for Excalibur—the lure of its magic like a familiar song. His hand clasped around the hilt just as Red slammed into his legs.

Still struggling with his tangled boots, Red was half

crawling and half diving across the floor, but he was moving fast enough to knock Galahad off balance.

Galahad lost his grip on Excalibur, and the sword skittered away as he hit the floor. Then Red was on top of him, pummeling him in a flurry of fists and elbows. It was all Galahad could do to bring his forearms up, shielding his head from the worst of the blows.

Red finally managed to kick off his boots. He leaped to his feet and lunged for Excalibur. Galahad, still dazed, grabbed Red's ankle, pulling him back to the ground. The two boys rolled across the throne room in a tangle of arms and legs. Red was stronger, but Galahad was smaller and managed to wriggle free of Red's headlock.

Regaining his feet, he sprinted across the throne room, knocking chairs as he went. He hoped they'd slow Red down. Across the Round Table, he could see Arthur, still asleep or worse, unaware of the chaos unfolding around him.

Galahad saw Excalibur, fallen half under the table. Without breaking stride, he bent and scooped it up. It was like touching a miniature lightning bolt, and he wondered how Red hadn't noticed the magic that now coursed through it. The sword seemed to pulse a welcome into his hand. The comforting weight that spoke to him in a way King Arthur's sword had not. He skidded to a halt and turned to face his foe.

Red had stopped running as well. To Galahad's dismay,

he had regained Arthur's sword.

"Why do you want Excalibur so badly?" Galahad asked between gasps, trying to catch his breath.

Red also breathed hard, but his eyes blazed. "I don't want a sword," he sneered. "I want *everything*. I want the birthright and the glory that *Uncle* Arthur stole from my mother."

He pointed an accusing finger at the king. "The great Arthur, who thinks he can rule by Merlin's lies. Well, there's still time to change what history will remember."

Red lowered his sword and charged.

Galahad backed into a defensive crouch. The two swords came together with a deafening clash that echoed around the throne room as the boys stood locked together, neither able to gain the advantage.

Red broke away first, bringing his blade in a low cut, but Galahad was quicker. He spun away, retreating around the table as Red followed, trading blows back and forth.

Neither sword struck their target. The great swords came together in violent clangs of steel on steel, sparks and splinters flying all around them as the combatants slowly circled the room.

Red surged forward again as they reached the throne. Galahad thought he saw a look of triumph in the other boy's eye, and prepared to raise his defenses, but Red suddenly turned away.

He leaped onto the Round Table, then onto the back of the throne. Toppling it over onto the broken windowsill, he vaulted out of the broken window, using the same escape tactic Galahad had used earlier that day.

Galahad ran to the window, but to his surprise Red was nowhere to be found. He had seemingly vanished.

A flock of crows burst overhead, and, with Excalibur firmly in his hand, Galahad could hear what they were saying. "The Two-Legger! Mustn't let him escape!"

There was a groan behind Galahad, and he whipped away from the window, still breathing hard.

The king had fallen forward from his chair, collapsing onto his hands and knees.

"Your Majesty!" Galahad cried, and rushed to the king's side. But before he could reach him, Arthur buckled to the ground, lying very, very still.

CHAPTER 49

Calib's large ears strained to hear King Arthur's breath, but he heard nothing . . . or there was nothing left to hear.

Gripping the ring tight, he bounded out from under the Round Table. "Galahad!" he cried. "The ring! You have to destroy it!" The boy was kneeling beside Arthur.

"He needs help," Galahad said, eyes filling with tears.

"*You* can help," Calib said, relieved that Galahad had been reunited with Excalibur. "This ring—it's cursed! It's corrupted by dark magic and has made the entire castle sick. If you destroy it with Excalibur, the spell will break. It'll save all those who are sick!"

To Calib's astonishment, the boy seemed to have understood every word.

"But I don't know if the king has the plague," Galahad said, reaching for King Arthur's wrist. "He's been poisoned."

Calib threw his gloved hands in the air, waving the ring. "It's a piece of Merlin's treasure, perhaps it will help! Please," he said, gesturing behind him at the other animals who stood there, mouths agape as they watched one of their own speak with a Two-Legger. "Many of our friends and family are sick— We need you!"

Galahad glanced at the open flagstone beneath the table, and Calib saw his face go white as he took in the sick animals. The Two-Legger nodded.

Calib held up the ring to the sword, and Galahad pointed the tip of Excalibur at it.

"Now what?" Galahad asked.

"Maybe you need to say something?" Calib offered.

Galahad gripped the hilt tighter, his knuckles white. "Heal!" he commanded.

Nothing happened.

"I don't think it works like that." Cecily's soft voice next to Calib's ear made him jump. She had crept up next to him and was staring with a hope that shone brighter than even the stars on the Lady's lake.

"How do you think it works, then?" Calib asked.

"Remember how the Lady said Galahad was denying his destiny?" she said, looking at the boy. "I think he has to let the magic *in* before he can let magic *out*."

Galahad puffed air out through pursed lips. He was looking like he might give up when Calib pulled gently on Galahad's socks.

The mouse placed an encouraging paw on Galahad's ankle.

"Let the magic in," Calib said both aloud and with his mind.

Galahad seemed to understand.

"Let me try again," he said, and closed his eyes.

Calib watched as the boy composed his face to show no emotion. His eyelids fluttered, and then he went still. Galahad looked as though he had fallen into a trance.

Glancing at the ring, Calib held his breath and waited. Nothing happened. And then—

A warm, yellowish glow began to illuminate the ring and sword.

All around, the animals murmured.

Calib felt a powerful magnetic pull between the two. Suddenly, the ring was wrenched from his paws by an unseen force. It hovered above the mice, spinning in slow circles. Long tendrils of black appeared around it, wrapping it like a black spiderweb.

"I can see it," Galahad whispered. Beads of sweat formed on his forehead. "The corrupted magic—but it won't let go!"

The Two-Legger was struggling. His features twisted with effort. Calib rushed over and leaped onto the boy's pant leg. Climbing quickly, he hurried down Galahad's arm to his clenched fist. He added his small paw to the hilt, lending his mouse-sized strength.

Galahad's eyes flew open. This time, there was focus in them, as sharp as lightning. With a last grunt, Galahad jabbed Excalibur toward the ring.

The yellow glow became a bright-blue flash, a brilliance so strong that Calib had to shield his eyes. He heard Galahad drop the sword to his side, and the ring clattered as he fell back onto the ground.

"It's done," Galahad said, sounding exhausted.

Calib slowly opened his eyes, blinking away dancing purple spots. As soon as he could see, he climbed down Galahad and hurried toward the ring. He stopped a whisker's length away from it, wondering if it was safe. But as he looked at the little wooden circle, certainty washed over him. The curse had been lifted—the ring wasn't even the same color anymore. Before it had been dark brown, but now the wood gleamed gold.

"It was never the mirror, but something from the lost

third treasure," Cecily said, marveling at the beautiful ring. "So whatever the treasure is, it must be wooden."

"How very . . . interesting," Mistress Pearl agreed.

From his vantage point on the Two-Legger floorboards, Calib could look down through the cracks into Goldenwood Hall's makeshift infirmary, where all of Camelot's sick creatures were slowly waking up.

A groggy Madame von Mandrake and Commander Kensington stirred from their feverish sleep.

"Maman!" Cecily cried out as she ran for the nearest tunnel to greet her mother. Warren and Macie blinked sleepily while Sir Alric called for some soup. And from the Two-Legger hallways, Calib heard loud voices and shouts—and laughter. The Two-Leggers were waking up, too!

All except one.

As Calib looked at King Arthur, lying still on the ground, he wondered if the cure had come too late.

Galahad reached for the ring and then placed it on the king's chest. Calib held his breath. For a moment, nothing changed, but then . . .

The King of England opened his eyes, his forehead furrowed in confusion. "I've had the most peculiar dream."

CHAPTER 50

Galahad helped Father Walter up from his sickbed.

"Red is a talented boy," the old man said, still quite weak from the curse. Galahad wrinkled his nose in disagreement but didn't say anything. "He could have done much good if he wasn't so focused on himself and his wants."

It had been a week since the events in the throne room.

The magical nature of the curse was still a mystery to the Two-Leggers, even though Galahad and Bors were working on continuing Red's translations. Camelot had been shaken to its very core. Many of the sick had suffered terrible dreams in their feverish state. But life was slowly returning to normal. The king, queen, and Sir Lancelot had all recovered, along with the rest of the courtiers.

Red had managed to escape the animals, though Arthur sent some knights to scrounge the countryside for his nephew. And Galahad had it on good authority that the Darkling Woods—and a particular family of foxes—was also tracking the traitor.

The old man's arms reached out, grasping for his cane. Galahad quickly placed it in his hands. Father Walter had recovered from the curse, but the fever had left him blind. There was no one left but Galahad who knew where all the herbs and medicines were located.

"Now that you've been promoted to squire, I suppose I'll have to find another aid soon enough," Father Walter sighed.

Galahad's heart was heavy as he helped the old man back to the infirmary. It was true; he had made squire. He looked down at his robes, now with Lancelot's crest emblazoned on his chest.

Galahad expected to be so proud of the moment he took the squire's oath, and in a way, he was. This was what he'd thought he wanted for a very long time, but now the victory came with the feeling that he was just doing what was expected of him, not what he thought was truly the best for himself or Camelot.

As they cleared the threshold into the apothecary wing, Galahad saw Sir Lancelot sitting on an empty bed, waiting for their arrival.

"Good morning, Father Walter," Lancelot said. "It's good to see you well again. I'm here to bring Galahad for a meeting of the Round Table. Do you mind?"

"Of course," the healer said. "I know these halls like the back of my hand."

Galahad followed Sir Lancelot into the kitchen garden. The boy looked down at his shoes, feeling terrible.

"Something told me I would find you here," Lancelot said slowly, "despite your promise that you would be at combat training today."

It was now or never. Galahad took a deep breath, but Lancelot interrupted.

"I have good news. Our scouts tell us the Saxon ships have been destroyed."

"How could that be?" Galahad asked, surprised. The enemies' sails had been spotted in the south mere days ago. Even before he'd regained his health, King Arthur had wasted no time preparing the castle for an attack.

"Some reports say they sank in the night, but there was no storm," Lancelot mused. "Strange business indeed."

The throne room was full of smiling and laughing knights when they arrived. Everyone congratulated one another. Visibly relieved, King Arthur was refilling his own cup of mead and toasting his knights. Queen Guinevere's smile was radiant as she greeted Lancelot and Galahad.

"Join us, good sirs," she said, beckoning them to approach.

King Arthur held up his glass to his second-in-command. "Lancelot, you have always been an extraordinary knight—a finer swordsman I never met. But I must say, your greatest accomplishment may be standing next to you now." King Arthur turned his attention to Galahad. "Galahad du Lac, could you please step forward?"

Lancelot placed a hand on Galahad's back and gently urged him.

"Thank you," Galahad said, suddenly shy. He had wanted recognition from the king for so long. But now that he had it, it felt less than what he expected somehow.

"Camelot still stands because of the actions of one," Arthur said. His voice resonated throughout the throne room, holding the rapt attention of the knights. "Not once, but *twice* have you protected us. The knights and I have discussed this at length, and though this is unprecedented, we agreed that you deserve nothing less . . ."

Galahad's heart felt like it was sprinting to catch up with his head.

"Galahad du Lac, will you take your place at the Round Table?"

King Arthur gestured to the seat to the right side of the throne—Merlin's seat, which had sat unoccupied since the wizard's disappearance. Many eyes widened in surprise.

No knight dared sit there, believing it jinxed. The last time someone tried, he promptly fell down some stairs and broke his tailbone. Nor had King Arthur ever offered the seat to anyone else, even Lancelot. Perhaps the king was finally accepting that Merlin would never come back.

Galahad felt his knees buckle, but he bowed quickly to stop from keeling over. His words felt like sticky cotton on his tongue.

"I— Sir— Th— I can't," he finished. "May I speak with my father alone, Your Majesty?"

The crowd was stunned. How could this boy refuse such a high honor from the king?

King Arthur only looked amused. He nodded. "Of course. This is a big decision for a young man."

Lancelot accompanied Galahad out of the throne room. Hushed whispers followed in their wake. On the other side of the throne room door, father and son sat down on a nearby bench.

"Is something the matter, son?"

The words spilled out of Galahad like a waterfall. "I know you're probably disappointed in me. But I don't think I can pretend to be something I'm not. The kingdom needs more than just fighters. Red is still out there, looking to take King Arthur down, and the Saxons have proven that they will try any means to capture the castle. We need thinkers. . . ."

His voice trailed off, and his heart clenched as Sir Lancelot observed him.

"I know you want me to be just like you, Father," Galahad began again. "But I don't—I don't want to be a knight. I want to be a healer."

Silence followed as Sir Lancelot looked at his son, as if seeing him with new eyes. Inside, Galahad was a storm of doubt. He braced himself for a scolding. How dare he embarrass his father in front of the king?

Then the knight did something surprising.

He gruffly hugged his son.

"You are the one who has saved Camelot twice now," Sir Lancelot said, his deep voice rumbling against Galahad's chest. "First, as a warrior, and then as a healer. I am so *proud* of you. Whatever you plan to do, I will support you."

Galahad couldn't believe his ears. "You mean, you're not mad at me?"

"Joining the Round Table doesn't mean you need to be a fighter. After all, Merlin was a wizard. I know that whatever you put your mind to, you will make it nothing less than extraordinary. It's in your destiny," Sir Lancelot said proudly.

Galahad felt a warmth inside that seemed to fill him from every corner of his heart. And he squeezed his father harder.

Together they reentered the throne room to take their places at King Arthur's Round Table.

CHAPTER 51

Calib never thought he'd be grateful to do his morning chores, but after everything that had happened in the past weeks, it felt like a treat not to have to worry about life-and-death situations. Even when those chores included cleaning the Goldenwood Throne until it "shone like a gold coin," as Commander Kensington had ordered.

As Calib polished until he could see his own reflection, he marveled at how quickly everyday life was returning to Camelot. The latest harvest of feverfew had been bountiful.

And with Mistress Pearl's aid, Madame von Mandrake was able to nurse nearly everyone back to health.

However, the plague had not left the castle unscathed. Scores of creatures perished to the white fever. Calib looked over to the new saplings that had been planted at the edge of the river in honor of Saffron, Edwin, and the others they had lost.

With the curse lifted and creatures getting well again, Commander Kensington had wasted no time in preparing for a feast to celebrate high summer. Tonight, Madame von Mandrake and Sir Alric were busy moving the banquet tables into the garden.

Calib felt a sense of renewed purpose as he wiped away the last smudge. For a moment, the mouse closed his eyes, letting the sun's warmth wash over him like a gentle embrace. It gave him the courage to face the one question that had been left hanging over him all week. He would ask it tonight.

"Commander Kensington?" Calib approached the mouse-leader late that night. Standing tentatively outside the council room, he scratched the white spot above his right ear.

"Yes, Calib?" Kensington was bent over the platter that served as the mice's Round Table, surrounded by scrolls from their library.

"I know you're busy," Calib said, creeping closer, "but

I was wondering if I could finish the final test—the wisdom challenge."

Kensington paused her note taking and put her quill down. She placed her paws together in a steeple and gave Calib a wry look, a cross between amusement and admiration.

"After all that's happened, I had forgotten that you never answered the final question in the Harvest Tournament challenge." She smiled at him. "Go on, what is your answer? What is most important to a knight: bravery, strength, or wisdom?"

Calib straightened his posture. This time, he was prepared. This time, he had an answer.

"The most important quality in a knight is kindness."

Kensington was stone-faced. Her fur had grayed since her recovery. "How did you come by that?"

"I was thinking about my father and mother, and about the others who have died defending Camelot," Calib said. "Bravery, wisdom, and strength are important, but it's not enough to just possess these qualities. Look at Red— He was brave, educated, and strong, but he doesn't deserve to be a squire of Camelot any more than a mushroom cap does. A true knight must use his gifts for the right reasons."

Kensington gave one of her rare, fierce smiles. "You will outshine us all yet, mousling."

"So I was right?" Calib asked, barely believing.

"Truth be told," Kensington said ruefully, "there is no right or wrong answer to the wisdom challenge—the only requirement is that the answer come from a place of virtue."

She unsheathed her sword from her scabbard and held it aloft. It was a great, shining blade, newly made by the hedgehog armorers to commemorate her reign. "Congratulations, Calib Christopher, you are now a squire. Kneel."

Calib felt all his fears release in one big whoosh. He dropped to his knees and lowered his head. The cold blade gently tapped his left and right shoulders.

"Rise, Squire Christopher," Commander Kensington said.

As he stood, he felt like a mouse reborn. Calib wished more than anything that his grandfather could see him now.

"Yvers would be proud of you," Kensington said, as if reading Calib's mind. She placed a paw on his shoulder. A shadow of sadness lingered over Kensington's face.

"It would have been Sir Owen's honor to train you," she said. "It was a promise he made to your father before he died. But seeing as both are no longer with us, I thought that you could train with me and Devrin, if you wished."

Calib's heart swelled larger than his rib cage could

contain. Impulsively, he gave Kensington a big hug. The commander stiffened, clearly not accustomed to such abrupt displays of emotion. She patted Calib's head awkwardly.

"There, there, no need to get carried away. I've just received word from a messenger lark that you may be interested in hearing. Barnaby and his crew have successfully sabotaged the Saxon fleet."

Calib froze. "His *crew*?"

"Yes. *His* crew. Erik Blackwhisker fell in the attack on the Saxons. Barnaby has been elected the new first mate to Captain Tristan." Kensington's voice was full of amusement. "He's had quite the adventure it sounds like. But he assured me that just because he's on the high seas does not mean he's forgotten his home."

Calib nodded solemnly, joy tangling with sadness at the same time. Joy for Barnaby, that he had discovered his true passion, but also feeling sad that he would not see his friend for some time.

"No doubt about it, there are trying times ahead," Commander Kensington said. Her eyes clouded, and Calib knew she was thinking of Red. "But tomorrow we will celebrate because that's all we can do when things are out of our control."

She smiled at Calib. "I have one last thing to give you, as Cecily recently informed me how you lost your sword."

Kesington brought out a long box. Calib's paw trembled as he opened it.

Inside was a near-exact mirror of his father's broadsword, but with some distinct differences. The hilt fit his paw perfectly. The crest of the Christopher sigil, the golden goblet with the sun rays shooting forth, was displayed larger on the cross-hilt.

"It is right to honor your legacy, but it is also good to make new a one," Kensington said. "And this sword deserves a name."

Calib thought about his father's sword, Darkslayer, named when the Darklings were the castle's main threat. But that wasn't the case anymore.

"Its name is Lightbringer," he said. He cut a fast figure eight in the air as Kensington looked on with pride.

Calib walked out of the council room with a light heart. Though war was brewing, he couldn't help thinking that everything was going to work out all right.

When he arrived at his dorm, the others were fast asleep. It was past midnight, but Calib wasn't sleepy. He sat on his bed and studied Lightbringer, memorizing every detail.

Calib trailed a paw over the Christopher crest. He'd always wondered what the crest meant; it was unusual to have such an ordinary household object as the symbol of one's family. When he'd asked his grandfather why the Christophers had chosen a goblet, Commander Yvers had always said that he would be told one day when the moment was right.

Calib's paw stilled. He stared at the golden Christopher cup with new eyes.

It was a gold that matched the throne he'd just polished.

His mind scrambled, remembering when Cecily had pointed out that if the ring was carved of wood, then the third treasure of Merlin must also be made of wood—a wood that shone like gold.

And the Goldenwood Throne . . . The animals always thought of it as a throne, but in reality, it was a cracked Two-Legger cup turned on its side.

The same kind of cup that represented the Christopher name.

Could it be that the Goldenwood Throne, the Two-Legger cup, was Merlin's missing third treasure?

Calib's whiskers twitched in excitement. It made perfect sense, and yet, how could the answer have been under their noses the entire time? Calib's suspicion burned a hole in his mouth. He had to tell someone!

Quietly, he slipped out of his dorm and ran across the hallway. It was late, but maybe Cecily would still be awake. He knocked on the door.

Dandelion answered, looking very put out in her pink nightcap. "What's so important that it couldn't wait until morning?" she asked, irritated. "I have a feast to help prepare tomorrow!"

"Sorry, Dandelion," Calib said. "But I need to talk to Cecily."

Dandelion yawned and shook her head. "She's not here."

"Where is she, then?"

Dandelion shrugged irritably. "I saw her earlier this evening with Mistress Pearl. Cecily looked a little upset, actually, but they were moving too fast for me to ask what was wrong."

"All right, I'll find her there," Calib said. "Sorry for disturbing your beauty sleep."

"I should say so!" she said before closing the door in his face.

As Calib rounded the corner to Mistress Pearl's chambers, he saw that the door was cracked open.

"Hello? Mistress Pearl?" Calib called out, knocking on the door. When there was no answer, he walked in. "I'm looking for Cecily. . . ." He trailed off.

Mistress Pearl's many clothes and scarves were scattered in disarray while scrolls and containers of makeup littered the floor. Lavender-scented oil from a broken jar seeped into the rug. A chilly breeze blew in from an open window above her desk.

He hurried over to close it, but as he was about to pull

down on the pane, the wind picked up. A parchment letter flew toward the window, but Calib grabbed it before it could slip out.

He finished closing the window, then tried to smooth out the crumpled letter. Calib's heart skipped. On the back of the letter was a broken wax seal with the letter *M*.

He held the letter to candlelight. Inside, there was only one sentence in thick black ink: *It's time.*

At the bottom, there was a bloodred paw print: the Manderlean.

For the second time that night, small mysteries—*details*, as Sir Alric would say— began to fall into place. But this time, the answer horrified Calib.

A traveling fortune-teller at Saffron's village had showed them Morgan's ring. Dandelion had said Edwin traded the lavender-scented oil to cover up the traveling bard's rotten egg smell.

Calib only knew of one creature who smelled like rotten eggs.

It was a creature forbidden from entering the castle, who would have needed to use makeup and a headdress or a nurse's mask as a disguise. A creature who had to kill a troubadour before the disguise was revealed. A creature they *knew* worked for the Manderlean: the traitor, Sir Percival Vole!

Calib's stomach clenched—even the name *Pearl* was similar to *Percival.*

It was all too clear now. A curse had been sent to Camelot at a time when the enemy knew the castle had no healers. Once the castle creatures were too weak and too desperate to look closely at new visitors, Percival had disguised himself as Mistress Pearl and presented herself as the only option.

But why had the Manderlean wanted Percival inside the castle?

The answer thundered into Calib, almost knocking him over: because they were searching for something. Captain Tristan had even *told* him that Manderlean was looking for a powerful treasure capable of harnessing the greatest magic of Britain.

The Manderlean wanted the Goldenwood Throne.

Calib took off faster than he had ever before. He ran as though owls and cats and sea monsters were chasing him, and he didn't stop until he entered the empty and darkened Goldenwood Hall.

Smoke from extinguished torches filled his nostrils, making him cough. He heard a panicked but muffled sound.

"Cecily?" he shouted into the darkness. His blood pounded in his ears as his arms reached for the closest torch and lit it.

The orange glow illuminated his worst fears: an empty stage. The Goldenwood Throne was gone!

In its place was a struggling Warren, bound and gagged. He was trying to shout with a rag wrapped around his snout.

"What happened?" Calib cried out, running forward to remove Warren's gag.

Rubbing his wrists, the gray mouse gasped for breath. "Percival Vole . . . He was here. . . . Took . . . throne . . . and took . . . and . . ." He stopped, tears leaking out of his eyes.

"Warren!" Calib wanted to grab him by the shoulders and shake the answer out of him. "What else did he take?"

Warren took in a deep, shuddering breath. "Cecily. He kidnapped Cecily."

ACKNOWLEDGMENTS

The voyage to Avalon would have been stormy indeed were it not for my first-rate plot navigators: Kamilla Benko and Andrew Harwell. Thank you for making this vessel a seaworthy one.

Much gratitude to the HarperCollins crew led by Admiral Rosemary Brosnan, Olivia Russo in publicity, Megan Barlog in marketing, Andrea Pappenheimer and her team in sales, Erin Fitzsimmons and Katie Klimowicz in design. And a special thank-you to Lindsey Carr, illustrator extraordinaire.

Much love to the forces of nature at Paper Lantern Lit: Lexa Hillyer, Lauren Oliver, Tara Sonin, Alexa Wejko, Adam Silvera, and Morgan York.

To my agent, Wendi Gu, thank you for being the wind in my writing sails.

To my husband, my family, my shield-maidens, and my coworkers, old and new: this year has shown me more than ever how lucky I am to know such marvels in my life.

Finally, I would like to thank my high school teachers,

in particular Mark Whittaker, Larry Boon, Brenda Yates, and Chuck Palmer. When I think back on those years, I realize the person I'm proud to be today originated there in your classrooms.